The Law of the Desert

BY BILL KEITH

Order this book online at www.trafford.com
or email orders@trafford.com

Most Trafford titles are also available at major online book retailers.

Note for Librarians: A cataloguing record for this book is available from Library
and Archives Canada at www.collectionscanada.ca/amicus/index-e.html

Printed in Victoria, BC, Canada.

ISBN: 978-1-4251-9206-8 (sc)

*Our mission is to efficiently provide the world's finest, most comprehensive book publishing
service, enabling every author to experience success. To find out how to publish your book, your
way, and have it available worldwide, visit us online at www.trafford.com*

Trafford rev. 09/01/2009

 www.trafford.com

North America & international
toll-free: 1 888 232 4444 (USA & Canada)
phone: 250 383 6864 ♦ fax: 812 355 4082

Forward

HAVING BEEN A voracious reader of Christian fiction since the age of 12, I am acquainted with most of the Christian authors and make Christian Book Distributors happy with all my purchases. Of the many books available I feel The Law Of the Desert ranks among the best. You will find yourself becoming more and more involved with the many characters and the inspiration they bring to the story. You will find yourself caught up in the hilarity and intrigue that is woven throughout, the first page to the last. This is a must read for lovers of westerns and those, for whom , this is their first Western novel. My brother Bill trooped off to Canada to attend Briercrest High School. He met his wife to be at the young age of 16. They married at the age of 19 and settled into the Tacoma area where they lived for 12 years and had three children. Bill sensed God's call into the ministry and it was only natural to return to the Briercrest schools to complete his education. Then he received a call to pastor a large rural church on the Saskatchewan prairie. He spent 7 good years until he returned to Briercrest where he served as dorm councilor and finally Dean of students. His career was interrupted when he received a diagnosis of Parkinson's Disease. He was eventually forced into retirement.

But God pours out many gifts on his children and the gift of writing was just one of the many gifts given to Bill. The Law of the Desert is Bill's second book (with a third in the hopper) and it will be a favorite for anyone who picks it up and opens it. Knowing that you will enjoy it and be as blessed as our family, you will want to have a box of Kleenex on hand for when you are rolling on the floor reading the hilarious portions and for when the Spirit of God moves you during those profound spiritual truths woven into the story line.

Claudia Branham

Prologue

O N SEPTEMBER FOURTH, eighteen eighty six the great Apache chief Geronimo and a handful of warriors surrendered to Major General Nelson Miles. This formally ended a campaign that had spanned many years, beginning with the arrival of the Spanish conquerors, and continued by the Colonists, then the pioneers. This grew into an overwhelming tide of men and women who were not satisfied until the nation stretched uninterrupted from sea to sea.

The Indians fought to stem this tide but as the years passed their numbers dwindled and they became weaker. The great war chiefs died or were defeated; The Buffalo, their main food source was destroyed. So they surrendered, bitter and dejected and forced to adapt to a way of life they neither understood or desired. Along with the acquisition of lands from the Indians, vast tracts of land were taken from the Mexicans from California to Texas, often by honest means but, sometimes not.

When the dust cleared the land had been won, but many enemies remained. This time good and evil squared off as men and women tried to settle and prosper in countless places throughout the West, The new warriors fought greed, hate, ignorance, illness, and one another, to see which side would prevail. Some battles were fought within the soul as individuals faced and struggled with the influences and temptations that would distract them from the noble aspirations that had guided their journey.

The battlefields included the mining camps, lonely desert trails and busy streets, or wherever the warriors happened to cross paths. One such warrior was Will Carter. His story begins in Yuma, Arizona territory in the late eighteen sixties. While his battles were fought in the usual places his greatest victories were won within his soul and often took place in the desert, where he loved to be. It was in the desert where he discovered a law that illustrated and illuminated the principles of life and enabled him to face and overcome the enemies that tried to destroy him. "I will pour out water on the thirsty land and Streams on he dry ground. I will pour out my Spirit on Your offspring and my blessing on your descendants" Isaiah 44:13

Bill Keith
101-1860
Penticton BC
V2A 7M6
Dec. 14,2000

Chapter I

T HE ARIZONA SKY was at it's blackest as the sentinels of the night blinked themselves out one by one. The moon had made it's departure and all that was left was one lone star, unwilling it seemed, to give way to the Monarch of the day sky without peeking one last time through the window at the young boy snuggled beneath his covers. After satisfying itself that all was well the star blinked out and retired for the day.

Almost immediately the sun began its appearance, heralded by a glow in the eastern sky that expanded into a warm curtain of light. As it moved Westward it chased away the darkness, and released tints and hues formerly unseen, but now free to play their symphony of color and motion as each stone and grain of sand, and rock formation displayed the rich and mysterious beauty the Creator had fashioned into them.

It also stirred the earth dwellers, one by one, from their slumber. The first to feel it's magic was a young fox. As the morning light washed his face he was suddenly seized by the pure joy of life and the wonder of his mothers tail, which being the closest thing to him began to experience the effects of his needle like teeth. Her short but painful response sent him scampering back to his corner to ponder the ways of life.

Next was an old Indian warrior, who had struggled most of the night with the knowledge that this was to be his last sunrise. He lay motionless thinking back to other sunrises and days of glory he had once known, and seen disappear in one short generation. It was hard to give up the past. Finally, with much effort, the old warrior summoned enough strength to raise his head and gaze fondly upon those gathered around him. Though determined not to let him die alone, they had long since succumbed to sleep and were oblivious to his voice of blessing as it rang briefly with the strength of love, then faded into an exhausted silence. The old man fought back a tear as his upraised hand fell and his head slowly sank into his pillow of wool. Then he slowly surrendered his last breath. He died easily as he had wished it to be.

The light continued it's course and overtook a weary doctor. He was grateful for the morning sun that soaked his painful body. He had fought a night-long battle helping a young mother bring her reluctant child into the world. This was the first of many sunrises for the child and though he had greeted his New World with indignation the Doctor hoped his days would be good. As for himself, just a few hours of sleep and he would be satisfied.

The curtain finally reached the town where a young boy lay safe under his blanket. The squeaking of an outhouse door split the morning air, joining the ringing of an axe, in a symphony of many sounds that announced the new day. The self important crow of an old rooster made it official, but the boy slept on, his ears deaf to the soft noises coming from across the hall. He slept as the sunlight began to flood through his window, awakening an exasperated fly that had been prisoner since the day before.

The boy didn't hear the angry buzzing and pops of the fly as it resumed its stupid attempts to break through the invisible barrier of glass that held it captive. He didn't hear his door open or the startled gasp, or the swat of the broom as the life of a small scorpion ended seconds after it abandoned it's sanctuary under the bed. "How in the world did that get in here?" The tone of his mother's voice revealed embarrassment that the security of her home had been breached. Then her attention shifted to the blanket covered form on the bed.

"OK Will...its time to wake up. We can't be late for church...You get up now and get at your chores!" Will finally began to stir as his mother's call, reinforced by the well placed jab of her broom, fought through the haze of his dreams, and coaxed him into consciousness. Poking his head from beneath the covers he smiled at her. Will was twelve years old and Helen Carter was the center of his world. To him she was the most beautiful woman in the world. She was tall and slender with long brown hair, and eyes that served as windows to her soul. She also displayed poise, and grace that made her welcome in any of the cliques that formed Yuma's society. She possessed unusual physical strength, and a faith that enabled her to look life square in the eye.

Her husband had died five years earlier leaving her to raise their son alone. They had planned to settle in San Diego where a good position awaited James Carter but their journey, which had originated in St. Louis, ended abruptly when his health suddenly began to fail. He then had only one goal, to provide for the future of his wife and son. He purchased a large house in Yuma, Arizona Territory and had it converted so she could operate a business taking in boarders.

Will had a vivid memory of his father. He was tall and muscular with sandy hair and steel blue eyes that were unable to conceal the enthusiasm with which he attacked each day. He also remembered helplessly watching as a strange illness attacked his father without warning, leaving him only a shell of the man he once had been.

Will had not yet fully come to terms with the loss of his father. There were too many unanswered questions, and the ever-present black hole in his soul, his father's absence created. Never the less he was able to recognize and overcome the fears and attitudes that if allowed to would overwhelm him. Even at his young age he respected the strength and guidance his mother provided. She confronted each day with courage and determination and it made him eager to carry his share of the load. Scrambling out of bed, and jumping into his overalls, Will headed for the barn to do his chores. It was a beautiful morning and he looked forward to the day.

He smiled as an angry Roadrunner scooted by him in hot pursuit of a Chihuahua, which sought shelter in a clump of bushes. Suddenly the bushes began to shake violently and a series of high-pitched yelps convinced Will that the poor dog was fighting his last battle. An instant later the Bird burst out of the bushes and ran for its life followed by the dog, which sauntered away with a triumphant gleam in its eyes. It was some time before Will was able to control his laughter. He had a spring in his step and it took no time to finish his work.

Sunday was his favorite day. After church he could look forward to his mother's fried chicken and apple pie. Then, as she settled on the veranda for the afternoon, he would join his best friend Ben at their secret swimming spot on the Colorado River. The morning flew by and soon Will headed for church to look for Ben. As he was hurrying around the corner of the building he almost ran right into him.

"Hey Ben, whatcha got?"

"Oh nothing, just an old lizzard."

"It's not a Gila Monster is it?"

"Nah!"

"Whatcha gonna do with him anyway?"

"Oh I thought I would take him to church and see if Pastor Tomkins could get him saved."

"How do you know he needs saving" Will asked.

"Why he is the meanest old lizzard I've ever seen...he took a chunk right out of my finger!" Will had no trouble with his friend's logic. He did think it best to take charge of the matter, so with a little persuading he convinced Ben that the lizard would be safer in his shirt pocket since it was deeper than Ben's. He carefully pinned his pocket shut to guarantee the lizard wouldn't get out and he and Ben took their favorite seats next to an open window.

As the service progressed Will forgot all about the lizard. He was totally absorbed in Pastor Tomkin's sermon. He could sweep his listeners along through the depths of sorrow and despair to the heights of joy and anticipation depending on his topic. This Sunday he was preaching on the crucifixion, describing the suffering of Jesus on the cross. The whole congregation groaned as they relived the anguish of Peter after his denial of Jesus.

More than one sob could be heard as the pastor painted a picture of rejection and remorse, and finally the possibility of forgiveness. Will sat with his eyes closed listening to the soft yet powerful words of the pastor. From early on he had been taught about God and His Son Jesus. He had asked Him into his life when very young. Now he was beginning to see the difference between knowing God and just knowing about Him. He had always viewed The Heavenly Father in terms of an earthly Father. This view, however was fading with each passing year since the death of his dad. This morning he felt an intense desire to know God better; to become closer to Him, but there were other forces competing for his attention. Presently he became aware of another stirring in his breast. Should he go forward? He had never felt this way before. Or was it really God? Suddenly he remembered the lizard. His hand went to his breast pocket, but he was too late.

The lizard wriggled free of Will's pocket and with a desperate leap landed on the back of Myrtle Brown's neck and immediately began digging its claws into her flesh. Will saw Myrtle tense up and knew he must retrieve the animal but before he could reach it, Myrtle shrieked and jumped to her feet. Her effort to dislodge the beast resembled an Irish jig combined with periodic deer like leaps. There were a couple of startled Hallelujahs as some assumed Myrtle was repenting but their joy turned to wonderment as they watched her desperately try to reach the aisle. Unfortunately her feet got tangled and she fell full length into the laps of Mr. and Mrs. Henderson who gasped in horror and jumped to their feet. Of course this dumped Myrtle onto the floor with a thud that jarred her passenger loose. He made the most of his opportunity and headed straight up the aisle, not stopping until he reached the mourner's bench. By now the congregation was a mass of confusion. The Hendersons stomped out in disgust as others gathered around Myrtle seeking to calm her down. Will and Ben jumped out the window and ran for their lives.

Pastor Tompkins, always the master of every situation, took control and brought the service to a close. The closing hymn seemed almost too appropriate this day; "All creatures of our God and King, Lift up your voice and with us sing Alleluia, Alleluia..." *(Francis of Assisi 1182-1226) His only respondent that morning was an irate lizard.

Will didn't enjoy any chicken this day, nor did he go swimming. He was banished to his room until sun up the next day. His mother did not believe in harsh discipline but when she asked Will what he was trying to accomplish in church he said "Why mom I was trying to get to know God better." To a twelve year old boy this made perfect sense and the lizard had nothing to do with what he was trying to accomplish. To a mother too busy to ask for an explanation it sounded like sass. Will was sentenced, deposited and secured in his room. A short period of freedom was granted so he could do his chores, which included stocking the woodbin. That was the worst punishment of all as it brought him to the kitchen, which was heavy with the aroma of chicken and dumplings left over from the supper meal. Later, when back in his room, Will heard a faint noise outside his door and upon investigating found a sandwich and cookies and a glass of milk, the fruit of his mother's mercy.

The next day all was forgiven. Helen Carter had long since learned to deal with a situation then let it go. She did find herself having to suppress her laughter several times as she remembered Myrtle's gyrations and the panicked exit of Will and Ben. Will walked to school with a warm heart. His spirit brightened further and his step quickened as he remembered this was a special day. Today they were getting a new teacher.

Miss Peabody, the former teacher, had abruptly resigned and departed for Los Angeles. It was noted that the oldest Dillon boy had also gone to LA. Will couldn't understand what she saw in Wade. As far as he was concerned the whole Dillon clan were mean spirited and shady. That is all but Mrs. Dillon and Wayne, the youngest son. A marked change had taken place in their dispositions around the time of the annual camp meeting. Now instead of avoiding Wayne when he and his mother came to visit he was glad to see him. Will was troubled though, by the fear which often shaded Wayne's eyes and the mysterious dark bruises which were sometimes present on Mrs. Dillon's arms and face.

Will's thoughts drifted away from the Dillon's. He enjoyed the solitude of his daily walk to school when he could allow his mind to wander and his eyes feasted on the beauty around him. He loved the desert warmth as it lifted off the hot sand and bathed his sun-browned skin. The air was clear and seemed to magnify the features of the mountains that bordered Will's world. Though they were barren and dry, not able to support foliage, they were never the less alive as the creeping shadows of the sun gave the illusion of movement.

The desert actually supported an abundance of life. Will's home was part of the Sonoran desert encompassing the Southern portions of Arizona and California and extending into much of Baja California and the Mexican state of Sonora. Will and Ben loved to explore their desert world and were familiar with it's inhabitants. He paused to acknowledge the little Elf owl that had fashioned it's home in the trunk of a huge Saguaro cactus. Their encounter, while brief, was important to Will and he considered the owl his friend. He wondered if the little owl missed him on Saturday and Sunday when he didn't pass this way.

The trees didn't grow tall but there were a variety of shrubs that provided ample color as well as shelter for the desert dwellers. The Hedgehog cactus, boasted flowers of beautiful Crimson. It also provided refuge for the ever-busy cactus mouse, snuggled in amongst the sharp quill like spines where it was safe from such predators as the hawks who hunted from the air and the four legged mammals who scoured the land for any beast small enough to be taken as a meal.

Other shrubs included Brittlebush, Blue Paloverde, and Cresote Bush. These provided a variety of colors that changed with the time of day and season of the year, thus making the desert, to the observant, a place of interest and challenge.

This day Will was so intent on his surroundings that he almost missed the little gateway into the schoolyard. His reverie was broken by Ben's greeting and he quickly corrected his course.

After a few words they joined a group of students who were engaged in earnest speculation on what the new teacher would be like. A couple of times Will caught sight of Mr. Miller, the Principle, who also taught the lower grades. It was obvious that he was in a state of agitation and Will could easily guess why. Mr. Miller was a fine teacher and an upright man, but he was also lonely. It was no secret that he desperately wanted a wife. His desperation had led him into many blunders and embarrassing situations in the past and it was apparent that he was setting the stage for yet another fall.

Presently the bell rang and the students expectantly made their way to their seats. Almost immediately Mr. Miller appeared with the new teacher. It was obvious he was flustered and also quite taken with the beauty of the young woman. The class sensed that something momentous was about to happen. When finally able to collect himself Mr. Miller called for the student's attention.

"Class" he said with the most official tone he could muster, "meet your new teacher Miss Lovely...I mean Miss Love!" Mr. Miller turned red and began to perspire as he realized his mind had been revealed, not only to the young lady, but also to the whole class.

He was aware of the laughter accompanied by the smirks and winks of the students. Somehow he must bring order and salvage the situation, if not for himself, for the young lady who was obviously very uncomfortable.

"Quiet class, we will have no more foolishness. Her name is Miss Love and she is not lovely." At this the class erupted in laughter. He had only dug himself deeper. Mr. Miller, completely undone, mumbled an incoherent apology to the stricken girl and stumbled out of the room.

It took only a moment for the new teacher to collect herself. She knew she must take control and decided it would be best achieved through discipline. She would let them know who the boss was.

"Alright class we're going to settle down...When you hear your name, stand at attention, look at me and say present." With that she began calling out each name row by row like a drill sargent. All went well until she got to Ben, who sat by a window.

"Ben Roberts."

"Present."

"Mr. Roberts look at me when your name is called."

"I am ma'am."

"No you're not, you're looking out the window... "I want all eyes forward when I'm speaking!"

Ben actually was looking at Miss Love but his face was looking out the window. Ben had an eye problem. They didn't exactly line up with each other. He had learned to adapt quite well under normal circumstances but stress always made the problem worse. Fixing her gaze on the red-faced boy Miss Love repeated his name.

"Present" he answered.

"Young man look at me!" The pitch and volume of her voice had gone up several levels and succeeded only in increasing Ben's distress. In an effort to satisfy the teacher Ben turned his head so his nose was pointed at her. Unfortunately she noticed his eyes were focused in the corner.

"Look at me!" Her exasperation caused Ben to snap his head around so his eyes could focus on her but his face was once again aimed out the window.

Will, unable to stand it any longer, jumped to his feet "Ma'am... can't you see his eyes don't line up, Ben has to point his face at the outhouse in the yard in order to see you at all." Will had not meant to imply anything but the thunderous response of the class coupled with the teacher's state of mind spelled disaster. With a menacing glare Miss Love reached for the oak rod standing against the blackboard and headed for the boys. Once again, within twenty four hours, they were forced to make their escape through an open window

They ran flat out until they reached their swimming place. Over the years the swirling current of the river had eroded the bank until it formed a cove about fifty feet in diameter. The water was calm and perfect for swimming. They wasted no time getting themselves into the refreshing water and were soon stretched out on the warm sand, soaking in the comforting rays of the sun.

Ben lifted himself up on one elbow and looked at Will. "I think that lady must be plumb crazy, even crazier than these silly eyes of mine." They stared at each other for a moment then Will gave Ben a little grin. "Ben, why are you looking across the river? Look at me when you look at me!" Their laughter washed away the last remaining traces of frustration.

Meanwhile back at school Mr. Miller had returned and dismissed Miss Love's class. He apologized to her and after hearing the account of her confrontation with Ben he explained about his eye problem. He was careful to add that Ben was a very intelligent and respectful boy. She was remorseful and humiliated and would have quit on the spot but Mr. Miller persuaded her to try again tomorrow. In the end they had a good laugh at the botched introduction and Ruth Love realized it had actually been a compliment. She also began to see a simplicity and sincerity in Mr. Miller that something from deep within wanted to respond to.

That evening Helen Carter noticed Will was exceptionally quiet as he stocked the woodbin and her wisdom told her he needed to talk. When Will turned around he spied a plate of cookies and two glasses of milk on the table. With a smile he slid onto his chair and faced his mother sitting across from him. He briefly told her of the episode with the new teacher. "Mom, why are people so mean to Ben? He's always being teased, even by church folks!" She quietly explained that people tended to judge others by how they look rather than by who they are. Will saw the qualities his friend possessed and because he knew and respected him he seldom noticed his eye problem.

"It's just not fair," Will protested, "Why does God allow bad things to happen to good people? Why did dad have to die? You shouldn't have to work so hard. Why do the Dillon's get away with mistreating the Indians? God could stop it all if He wanted to."

Helen Carter chose her words carefully. "Yes, God could stop it and He will some day. Don't forget, when He made the world and put people on it everything was good." She explained that it was mans disobedience that had allowed bad things to come into the world. "Some day God will remove the bad, and until that time He promises to help us when ever we need it."

Will thought quietly for a moment. "I sure hope He knows what He is doing." Mrs. Carter smiled at her son and assured him that God did know what He was doing. Will was thoughtful as he finished up his chores. He was growing up. He had observed and experienced enough of life's hardships to realize he lived in a world that could be ruthless. One needed only to look at the once prosperous Pima Indians who lost their water to the greedy white man, and now lived in poverty, to see how unfair life could be. On the other hand the love and compassion displayed by his mother and others around him who practiced true integrity, set an example and provided a course for him to follow.

Will thought again of the new teacher and her treatment of Ben. His resentment began to melt as he considered how she must have felt. He determined to give her a chance to prove herself before he passed judgment on her.

The next day, seeking to prepare herself and devise a strategy for establishing herself with the class, Miss Love arrived early. She stopped cold as her eyes fell on the black board. Someone had drawn a picture of a cross eyed boy tipping over an outhouse. Inside it was a wild looking lady, eyes wide open in terror. Miss Love began to cry, then she started to laugh as the humor of it sunk in. She knew how she would approach the class. She also determined to keep her eyes open until she discovered which of the students was so artistically gifted. Her first act that day was to apologize to Ben in front of the class, then she complimented the mysterious artist for doing such a fine job. The picture was left on the board for the whole day and became a bridge between teacher and class.

It wasn't long before Ruth Love completely won the students over. She had a special respect for Ben as she recognized his integrity and the kindness that he demonstrated. She also noted his academic ability and determined to do all she could to aid him in the one area where he struggled, his ability to read.

Will liked school and was a quick learner. He was also a keen observer and didn't fail to note the friendship that was developing between Ruth Love and Richard Miller. All in all the school year was progressing quite well. Things would have been perfect if it were not for one problem. His name was Todd Dillon. Todd assumed it was his duty to make life miserable for those around him. For some reason he seemed to concentrate his efforts on Will and his two friends. His taunting of Ben never seemed to end and he took every opportunity he found to bully Running Bird.

Running bird was a Pima Indian. His small lithe frame combined with his swiftness of foot had earned him his name. Orphaned at birth, he was given to the Ohares, owners of the large general store in Yuma. Running Bird's grandmother had brought him to them when he was eight years old when she realized she could no longer care for him. They loved him and gave him the best of what they had. In return, He loved them and was filled with gratitude but he could not rid himself of the feeling of being displaced and out of his element. He and Will had become friends and along with Ben they formed a threesome that provided Running Bird with much needed companionship and acceptance.

The only flaw in this arrangement was the intrusion of Wayne Dillon. The Dillon's had mistreated Running Bird and his Grandmother and he held a grudge against them. It really didn't matter to Running Bird that Wayne hadn't been involved. Wayne was a Dillon therefore he shared the blame.

Will refused to respond to the constant baiting from Todd, not wanting to fight. Unfortunately Todd saw this as weakness on Will's part, and intensified his attacks. Will finally came to the place were he would take no more. Things came to a head during noon break one day. Todd walked by Running Bird who was eating a jam sandwich, grabbed it and smeared it all over his face. "Now little red skin you look normal, Indians never have clean faces."

Running Bird jumped up to retaliate but before he could reach Todd, Will stepped in between. Todd gave Will a smirk and opened his mouth to say something. He never got a word out, nor did he see the fist that laid his nose flat against his cheek. Stunned, he stood legs apart, head down as the blood streamed from his nose, drench-ing his shirt. Then things began to get dark and his knees buckled.

When Todd regained consciousness Ruth Love and Mr. Miller were bending over him. He was ordered to lie still until they stopped the bleeding. Todd was overcome with rage and humiliation. "You cheater," he shouted at Will, "I'll get even with you!" He began to abuse and threaten Will, who's only response was to take a couple of steps toward Todd.

"Shut up Todd, and if you ever mess with Running Bird again it wont be your nose that I break."

At this point Mr. Miller told Running Bird and Will to go home. He had sent for Mrs. Dillon and was afraid Thad Dillon, Todd's fa-ther, might also show up.

Todd missed a week of school. When he did return his behav-ior was changed. He was quiet and withdrawn, keeping to himself. Ruth Love was relieved and grateful that the class room was back to its normal level of order. She could not shake a sense of foreboding, though, as several times she observed Todd casting murderous looks at both Will and Running Bird. She had heard about the Dillon fam-ily and determined to inform Helen Carter of her concerns.

As for Will the matter was settled. Refusing to worry about Todd, he went his way and got on with life. As the weeks turned to months, things settled down and life took on a predictable routine. The only exception was the occasional shooting or brawl that took place in the rougher part of Yuma.

Younger than twenty years old, Yuma was a diverse town. It possessed the best and the worst of humanity. There was a core of upstanding folk intent on building a prosperous and secure com-munity where everyone would feel safe and accepted. There were also those who cared little for law and order and were not above any act if they thought they could get away with it and it would bring benefit to them. Consequently there were parts of town that Will and his friends were forbidden to enter. Will was obedient to this rule, but one night a series of events caused him to venture into a dangerous part of town. What resulted was a situation that brought long term repercussions.

Chapter 2

I T HAPPENED THE night of the semi annual Ladies Society Music and Variety Night. This was one of the nights when those considered to be gifted, were able to show off their talent. This event was attended by a broad spectrum of people and for many different reasons. Pastor Tomkins attended because he was expected to and his wife made sure that he did. The Mayor attended because it impressed people and got him votes. The sheriff and town council attended because their wives made them go and it was to their advantage to pretend to go voluntarily.

Then there were the young men of Yuma. Those who were married were there because they had gone before marriage to impress the girl they were wooing and they simply didn't know how to get out of it and preserve domestic peace and tranquillity now that they were no longer free. Those who were not married were there for the same reason the married ones had attended when single. The only difference was that they were still of the illusion that once they had won the hand of their lady fair they would somehow be exempt from the expectation they were naively establishing.

Will was there because there was nothing better to do and he knew something interesting would happen. It always did. If nothing else it was entertaining to watch the young women, who considered themselves the cream of Yuma's society exert their absolute domination over their unfortunate husbands who had no choice but to play the role that had been foisted upon them-that of appreciaters of fine art and culture.

Along with Will were Ben and Running Bird. This evening Wayne was not present which made Running Bird happy and he shared the expectancy of his friends. Accompanying the three boys was one more member of the group. Because "Happy" was of the canine variety his owner made him sit outside under an open window. Ben hung his arm out the window and held on to Happy's leash. Now "Happy" was not the most appropriate of names for the dog. His had not been a particularly happy life. Until Ben had taken him in he had been on his own. He wore the scars of many battles and close scrapes. He possessed only one complete ear, the other one having been chewed to a quarter of its original size. His tail had suffered a similar reduction in length, and he had a permanent limp as a result of a bad experience with a freight wagon.

Happy also had a bad attitude. His countenance was sullen, his eyes constantly on the move seeking potential danger. His usual expression seemed to say "leave me alone and we'll all be better off." He avoided other dogs, hated cats, worshipped Ben and tolerated his friends. Needless to say he was not particularly enjoying the festivities. The boys, on the other hand were becoming quite taken with the proceedings, unfortunately for the wrong reasons.

For some time they had been entertained by the expressions of misery on the faces of several of the husbands. At regular intervals an irate wife would deliver a well placed elbow or foot, thus returning a dozing husband from blissful slumber to consciousness. An involuntary snort or an incoherent word, or a spontaneous kick would often punctuate his return. This would always draw a glare from his wife that struck fear into his soul as he meekly slunk down in his seat.

Presently the boy's attention was attracted to the presentation then in progress. Myrtle Brown fancied herself to be a fine soprano. Her most striking asset however was her ability to produce music at a volume unequalled by any other. When she let it all out she could clear a building of every rodent within the confines of its walls. Thus as a precaution several of the men, including Pastor Tomkins, had packed cotton in their ears before they left home.

The song of choice spanned the scale from the lowest to the highest of notes. She stood, hands folded in front of her swaying body with her head tilted up gathering steam for the finale. The boys sat transfixed, fascinated by the sound she produced and in awe of the oscillations of her throat. After staring for a time Running Bird said, "Why she looks like she's trying to swallow a fish that's too big to go down".

This brought a sudden outburst of laughter from the back corner, as several of the husbands who heard his comment were unable to suppress their pent up misery. To make matters worse Happy had set up a high pitched wail as if trying to out do Myrtle. Will and Running Bird were doing their best to stifle their laughter but it was hopeless. Consequently they were taken by the collar and put out the back door. Ben made his escape through the window.

Though they had been ejected they were not about to leave. The next item on the program was Mr. Henderson on his violin. In Will's mind that was the only thing that could equal Myrtle's voice. Mr. Henderson played with an enthusiasm unmatched by anyone, especially when combined with his unique ability to produce sounds that had never before been produced on a violin. While beyond description, suffice it to say, when within range it caused your scalp to crawl and your teeth to hurt. The melody, while usually present, was never dominant.

Once again things were getting out of hand. Will and Running Bird were doubled over with their hands clapped over their mouths. Ben was holding Happy's mouth shut and a love struck Tomcat was approaching the music hall entrance. Each time one of Mr. Henderson's special sounds came forth the cat, mistaking it for the love call of an infatuated feline, gave a little sideways hop and skipped a couple of steps forward. Just as the cat reached the door he was favored by a mighty moaning screech from the violin. Slipping through the door the cat responded with an enthusiastic meow of it's own. Unfortunately this alerted Happy to the cat's presence. Happy jerked free of Ben's hold and was off after the cat.

Ben looked in the window just in time to see the cat streaking up the aisle followed by the enraged dog. Mr. Henderson stood transfixed in horror as the cat clawed it's way up his body and upon reaching his shoulder, dug in and hung on for dear life, his front legs clinging to the mans neck. Happy was briefly distracted when a man grabbed his leash thus giving the cat opportunity to make his escape. His path of retreat took him across the dessert table piled high with the fruit of the ladies efforts. The first landing took care of the sandwich assortment, scattering them everywhere and providing the cat a little respite as Happy stopped long enough to sample the fare. The cat's second leap demolished the neat rows of little cups of punch some lady had painstakingly arranged beside the punch bowl. This provided a rather soggy launching for the now terrorized projectile that cleared the porch with a final leap and fled into the darkness followed by the dog and three excited boys.

The chase took them through gardens and yards, and over hedges. Running Bird became tangled in a loaded clothesline and for a brief time it looked like a fight to the death. He was finally able to break lose but his efforts to free himself left the laundry in a tangled heap. The next morning a puzzled and angry lady re-washed the clothes. Running Bird was faster than Will and Ben and they were soon out distanced and forced to keep track of the chase by the sounds ricocheting back to them. Once they heard the shattering crash of something going through a wall. Then they heard the out-cry of human pain and of panic filled, chickens flapping their wings and squawking, as the boy exited the chicken yard. Shortly after that they detected the startled yelp of dogs then angry barking. Running Bird had stumbled into the middle of a pack of stray dogs.

Toward the end of the chase the angry voice of a man rang out, "I'll teach you to run through my lettuce!" This was followed by the roar of a shotgun and the high pitched wail of a young Indian boy. Will and Ben finally caught up with Running Bird, who looked very much the worse for ware. His face displayed no humor as he tried to reach the little pieces of rock salt that had been deposited in his posterior by the angry lettuce grower. It was apparent that the cat had eluded Happy. Ben was sure he would go home so they decided to return to the concert. It was then that they discovered they were in a very dangerous part of town. Jumping to their feet they headed for safer territory.

Will assumed his friends were following him but each boy had gone his own way. Consequently He found himself alone in an area he had never been. Walking quickly, carefully keeping himself in the shadows, he soon came to a street that contained many brightly-lit buildings, including several gambling halls and a few run down looking hotels and saloons. They spewed forth a steady din of piano music accompanied by the clatter of dice and the noise of roulette wheels. Each time the dice stopped or the wheel came to rest Will could hear a combination of exuberant cries from the winners and curses from those who lost.

Yuma was a major gathering and distribution point for goods destined for military posts in Nevada, Utah, and New Mexico. Goods that came from California around the Baja Peninsula to Port Isabel were then shipped up the Colorado by riverboat or over land by freight wagon. With the goods came employment and with jobs came men. There were Teamsters, Miners, Prospectors, Sheepherders, and Cattlemen. For every honest man there was at least one who wanted to rob or swindle him. The latter kind seemed to be dominant in the establishment before Will.

Will could not resist the temptation to look in through a window and was soon engrossed with the activities taking place. He noticed that the saloon girls were quick to attach themselves to the men who were winning or who demonstrated any kind of generosity, thus exposing themselves as an easy mark. Will scanned the crowd, fascinated with the different ways the people were dressed. obviously every strata of society and financial position was represented. They all seemed to have one thing in common, a sense of freedom to indulge themselves as they wished with no worry of danger or reprisal or need to give account. The morals and values they held within their normal circles of society were for the moment set aside. They would indulge their baser instincts tonight and don the garb of respectability on the morrow.

Will was suddenly jolted back to the reality of his position when his eyes fell upon Thad Dillon, a man he both feared and loathed. Thad was cruel and ruthless; His cruelty often left its mark on his wife. Will was also reminded of the fear he often saw in the eyes of Wayne Dillon, a fear he kept inside, unable to expose even to Will who was the one person he counted as a friend.

Thad Dillon was with another man whom Will had never seen before. He was big and roughly dressed and his face revealed a ruthlessness that matched that of his companion. They seemed to be watching someone or something with great interest. Will followed their eyes and what he saw made him tense with surprise and dismay. Seated at a table with three other men and obviously deeply involved in a poker game, was Nathan Penny. Nathan was a resident of Helen Carter's boarding house and was, as far as Will knew, an upstanding man who would not frequent this type of establishment. It was obvious that he was winning big and it was also apparent to Will that Thad Dillon and his friend were interested in his winnings.

Will continued to watch, wondering what to do. Before long the game broke up and Nathan gathered up his winnings and prepared to leave. He didn't notice the two men slip out the side door but Will did, and he knew he must do something quickly. Running around to the front of the building he came face to face with Nathan who looked at him with shock. "What are you doing here?"

"Never mind that now, we have to get out of here," answered Will, "there are two men waiting to rob you."

Nathan Penny's face turned pale and his jaw set. The lines of his features hardened and Will could see that he was angry. They both knew they were being watched and that the two men would be armed. Grabbing Will's arm he pulled him into the saloon and found a table in the corner where he sat him down. He instructed Will to stay put then walked over to a young cowboy standing at the bar. After speaking briefly to him he returned to the table where Will was sitting.

The young cowboy left and in less than ten minutes returned. Turning to Nathan he gave him an almost imperceptible nod. "Alright Will, We're going out the back door and we're going to get on the horses that are waiting for us. Head for home as fast as you can and don't stop for anything. I'll be right behind you." With that they walked to the door. Nathan took a quick but careful look out into the alley. Then taking Will by the arm he said "lets go!" and pulled him out the door and almost threw him onto the horse. As he mounted his own horse he shouted for Will to ride and they were off at a run. They had gone no more than a block when Will heard shooting. Plastering himself to the horse he dug his heels in and let it have it's head. In no time Will was in familiar territory and soon reached his home. It was only then that he noticed his companion was not with him.

At the sound of Will's arrival Helen Carter came out to investigate. She gave her son a shocked look and opened her mouth to ask what on earth was going on, but before she could say anything Nathan Penny came pounding up the street. Jumping off his horse he shook Will's hand vigorously and turning to his mother said, "Mrs. Carter, your son saved my life this evening. He's a boy to be proud of, and I'm mighty grateful."

"Do you mind telling me what is going On?" she asked. "The last I saw of my son he was disrupting a musical concert."

Will blushed and looked down and Nathan grinned. "I guess we had better go inside and have a talk."

At his mothers request Will explained his presence at the gambling hall and expressed his surprise at finding Nathan there. Nathan explained that his position with the mining company required him to sometimes go into places he would not otherwise frequent. Tonight he was there because a man he had been following led him there and his lose tongue had imparted much valuable information. The fact that he had won at poker was simply luck. He asked Will and Helen to trust him. There were some things he was not at liberty to tell them as it would jeopardize his work and put him in danger if it leaked out. He had confidence in them but didn't want to add unneeded responsibility to the concerns they already had.

Nathan was concerned about Will. He was convinced Thad Dillon knew the boy had warned him. A couple of his friends had chased them off but Nathan was sure Dillon and his partner would be back. He'd had scrapes with him before and knew he would not rest until he punished Will for ruining his plans. The next day Nathan talked to Sheriff Moore. Though there was not enough evidence to lay charges the sheriff wasted no time in hunting Dillon down and threatened him with grave consequences if he so much as looked sideways at anyone or stepped out of line in any way. A few days later the two left town.

Will was relieved but he was still uneasy. He had seen the baser side of life and the dangers it posed. Part of his childhood innocence was lost as he entered onto the path to manhood.

Over the next several weeks Nathan and Will became friends. It was a friendship driven by mutual respect. Along with his respect for Will Nathan was determined to protect and prepare the boy for the danger and challenges he would eventually face. As for Will, his need for someone he could respect and count on, and who he could share his innermost thoughts with was met in Nathan Penny.

Helen Carter was troubled to see her son growing into manhood in only his thirteenth year and feared losing the closeness they enjoyed. She also understood his need for a father figure and reluctantly but thankfully stood aside, refusing to interfere with the relationship that was developing. Nathan decided it would be wise to expand Will's education beyond the realm of the academic, and with the hesitant permission of his mother, Will entered a new chapter in his life.

It was also a new beginning for Helen, and something she had lost was once again part of her life, the friendship of a man. For the first time since her husband's death she felt at ease around a single gentleman. She sensed his genuine respect and concern for her well-being and looked forward to his visits. As the weeks passed and the friendship grew she began to wonder, with mixed feelings, what her future held.

Chapter 3

WILL LOOKED IN awe at the star filled sky. He had never seen so many stars. Suddenly he stiffened, seized momentarily by panic, as a shower of meteors burned themselves out directly over his head. Nathan smiled at the reaction of his friend and savored the cup of coffee that warmed his hands. He sipped it slowly getting the benefit of every bit of its warmth. They had made camp early, before dark, lighting only a small fire and putting it out as soon as their supper was cooked. They wanted no light to reveal their location. Earlier in the day they had spotted dust a few miles behind them, and while not sure they were followed they were taking no chances.

The anticipation on Will's face made Nathan smile again. He had business that would take several days and as it corresponded with Will's Christmas break he saw it as an opportunity to introduce him to some of the desert's secrets and mysteries that could mean the difference between life and death. Leaving Yuma they had gone straight to Picacho where they had spent a couple of days. Nathan spent several hours each day with mining officials while Will fought boredom at the home of Victor and Ruth Rojas. It simply wasn't safe for Will to be on his own. Nathan suspected Thad Dillon was in or around Picacho. Even if he wasn't he had friends who were. Besides, it seemed every other man there was a thief and would be only too glad to rob him. Victor Rojas was a good friend of Nathan and agreed to keep Will out of harm's way.

The Rojas' didn't know how to worry but were very good at relaxing, consequently they slept the afternoon away while Will paced the floor and resisted the desire to explore the town. He was relieved when they departed and headed into the desert toward the Chocolate Mountains.

Nathan was checking several cites where claims had been filed, looking for evidence of fraud or foul play. Several claims had changed hands under mysterious circumstances along with the disappearance of several men over a span of two years. Nathan was assigned the task of solving the mystery.

Now they were in the middle of the desert, all alone, or so they hoped. Nathan had made camp on the highest spot he could find and as a result they could see for miles in nearly every direction as the moon illuminated the landscape.

As his eyes searched the night, Nathan talked to Will about the desert. He told him how to locate water by observing the plant life, and which animals lived close to water and those that didn't. He described the rock formations that would be most likely to trap water and store it. Will listened with keen interest. The next several days would be proving days for him and he didn't want to disappoint his teacher.

As Nathan talked a sense of well being stole over Will and it became hard to focus on what his teacher was saying. Then he ceased to hear him altogether as his eyes closed in sleep. Nathan smiled and put an extra blanket over him. Then he quietly slipped out of camp and into the quiet chill of the desert night.

Will woke up before dawn, his body complaining and demanding relief from its cramped inactivity. There was no place that didn't hurt. He was not used to being on a horse for so many hours at a time, nor was he accustomed to sleeping on the hard ground. In spite of the pain Will felt a sense of satisfaction. The soft flesh of youth was being replaced by muscle. Will walked around for a while wondering where Nathan was and what was in store for him this day.

Once again his attention was drawn to the pre-dawn sky. He was overwhelmed by a sense of total solitude, as if the Creator, with a big brush, was painting the new day. He felt like a mere speck in the vastness of creation. How could he ever find his way? How could he ever be found in such a vastness?

Suddenly it was as if the Creator was splashing the multi-colored spender of this desert morning across the eastern sky for the pleasure of him alone. His heart sang with gratitude and he bowed his head in thanksgiving. Will had never felt so complete in his life and he vowed never to wander away from such a heavenly Father. Soon the colors gave way to the light of the new day and Will began to enjoy the sun's warmth.

The rattle of a stone caught Will's attention and to his relief he saw that Nathan caused it. Walking up to Will he smiled and handed him a revolver and holster. "Starting today you're learning how to handle a gun...but first we're going to have breakfast." With that they set about making their morning meal.

As they ate Nathan began talking. Will questioned the need for a gun but Nathan reminded him that he had made at least two enemies who had no conscience. In addition South Western Arizona and California were teeming with men who had learned to kill during the Civil War. Having nothing to go home to when the war ended, many had come west to find their fortune. For some it mattered little if it belonged to someone else or if they had to take it by force.

Nathan further explained that a gun kept in plain sight was more effective than one that was hidden. If hidden it was no deterrent but a person would think twice about challenging a man knowing he had a gun. "Never draw a gun unless you intend to use it and never use it unless there is no other way. Walk away from trouble if you can. Remember, never let anger or pride influence what you do in any situation."

There was another danger also. Though technically at peace with the Indians, the white man had been unfair and sometimes brutal in subduing them and as a result there was much resentment. There were always a few Indians who hid themselves in the remote places and waged war against the white man.

Nathan taught Will how to hide a trail and how and where to travel without being seen. Knowing how to use a gun was only a small part of survival. You must also know how to avoid the enemy.

The rest of the day was spent in practice. After having Will put the gun belt and holster on, he made him practice drawing the gun over and over until he could do it with a smooth and uniform motion. He then had him practice drawing and squeezing the trigger. This was done with no bullets in the gun and was intended to teach Will to fire the gun with accuracy.

After satisfying himself that Will would not shoot himself in the foot he had him load the pistol and practice slowly drawing and firing. He took him step by step until it felt natural and comfortable. By mid afternoon Nathan was satisfied that Will could handle the gun safely. Now it was time to see if he could hit what he aimed at. "Alright Will lets see if you can hit that big stone." He indicated a stone about the size of a sheep and about fifty feet away. With an easy motion Will drew and fired. Nathan stared mouth open in disbelief. Will had hit it dead center. "Do it again."[1] In response Will drew and fired three shots all within a circle of six inches and dead center of the stone.

Nathan could not believe what he was seeing. It was obvious that Will was a natural. Nathan pointed out target after target and Will kept hitting them. His accuracy finally began to diminish as Nathan picked smaller and more distant targets. Nathan's excitement was tempered with some misgivings. Had he done his friend a service? He spent the rest of the day talking to Will about the potential dangers and the temptation to use his gun hastily or for the wrong reasons.

Will had no desire to shoot another person and assured Nathan of this fact. He also expressed doubt in his ability to use a gun even in self-defense. After they had talked the matter over for some time and Nathan saw the spirit that motivated Will, he assured him of his confidence that he would do the right thing if and when the need presented itself.

The next several days were spent on horseback. With each day Will became more comfortable and at home in the desert. He was also taking on a toughness that enabled him to ride several hours without having to rest, or quench his thirst. He was learning to conserve the moisture and energy in his body and stretch himself to his limit.

Nathan wasn't concerned for Will's physical safety and well being only. He had come to recognize and respect the qualities he saw in him. He knew of the dangers and influences that had turned other once positive young men onto a path that ended in personal ruin. For this reason he was determined to point out the pitfalls. That night by the campfire, Nathan asked Will if he knew the story of Crazy Tom Pound. Will confessed he didn't but he asked Nathan to tell him the story. Nathan began.

As a young man Tom Pound had come out West leaving his wife and small child behind until he could afford to establish a home and bring them out to join him. He was ambitious and hard working and soon had a good amount of money saved. In fact he needed only a little more before he could send for his wife and son.

About that time he began to notice people who had struck it rich, some by finding gold and some by other means not so honorable. He saw them indulging in a life that seemed attractive, and his goal of reuniting with his wife became secondary to his quest for riches.

His letters became less frequent as his obsession grew. He finally did strike it rich. With prosperity came friends who helped him spend his money. His wife and son retreated further into the recesses of his mind until he stopped writing and barely thought of them at all.

One morning he woke up to find his fortune gone along with his friends. It was then that he remembered his wife and son.

He desperately wanted to see them but he was too ashamed to write and tell them what he had done. He decided he must find another gold mine and set out to do just that. He told himself "just a small strike", but he never found it. Loneliness and guilt finally drove him crazy.

Now he wonders from place to place dressed in rags with everything he owns on the back of his old donkey. You'll know him when you see him because his only greeting will be, "Just a small strike."

As he finished his story Nathan looked over at Will and knew it had struck a chord deep within his being. He watched as he quietly rose to his feet and walked into the darkness. Will didn't know how to deal with the feelings he was experiencing. He felt an overwhelming compassion for the son of Crazy Tom. In fact he knew just how he felt because he had been deserted by his father also. He was once again experiencing the loss and loneliness, and the anger he thought he had dealt with a long time ago.

He knew he couldn't blame his dad. He had not chosen to leave his wife and son as Crazy Tom had. Suddenly it dawned on him that Crazy Tom hadn't intended to desert his son either. He had been distracted and lured away from his purpose. He began to feel compassion for the man who had lost everything including his son and wife. Will slowly returned to camp and sat down by the fire. Nathan kept quiet, realizing his friend would talk about it when he was ready.

The next day they were on the trail early. Will was quiet all morning and Nathan left him to his thoughts. Suddenly Will spoke. "That foolish farmer!"

Pulling his horse up and swinging around Nathan said "what?"

"I said that foolish farmer, that foolish farmer! You know, the farmer God said was a fool".

"What in the world are you talking about?" Nathan regretted the irritation he heard in his voice but Will didn't seem to notice.

Will told the story of the foolish farmer Pastor Tomkins had preached about. He had become very rich but had not been grateful nor had he shared his wealth with those in need. Instead he planned only how he could best keep what he had for himself. When God called him to account he lost everything including his own soul.

Nathan was dumbfounded. He marveled at Will's insight and his ability to think. Without a word Nathan turned his horse around and they continued on their way, neither one disturbing the thoughts of the other. They continued on for several hours, stopping only long enough to have a quick lunch. Finally toward evening they came to a place sheltered by a low rocky bank and set about to make camp.

"Hey look, those rocks have gold in them!" Will was trying to hold back his excitement.

After a quick look Nathan chuckled and explained the difference between fools gold and the real thing, then he had an idea. "It's kind of like Crazy Tom or the foolish farmer."

"What do you mean?"

Nathan explained that if you go after the wrong things you will never be satisfied and going after the right things for the wrong reasons has the same result. Both Crazy Tom and the foolish farmer were seeking what was legitimate but for the wrong purpose. Nathan continued "So it boils down to this, find your purpose, live true to that purpose, and remember it will always involve helping others."

Will had only one question, "How do you find your purpose?" Nathan smiled, "That's easy, the one who created you did it with a purpose in mind, ask Him." Will's face lit up and Nathan smiled. This trip had been far more profitable than what Nathan had hoped for. Tomorrow they would go home.

The next day as they neared Yuma, Nathan pointed out that many a prospector had passed over a fortune because he only had eyes for gold. There were other metals and minerals that could bring wealth but they went unnoticed by those who had only one thing on their mind.

Will got the point, and summed it up by saying "So we should be careful to keep our eyes open for every opportunity that comes our way."

Nathan nodded as they topped a little rise and saw the Colorado river in the distance. It was good to be coming home.

Chapter 4

WHEN WILL AND Nathan arrived at the Yuma ferry crossing the first person they ran into was the sheriff. He informed them that Thad Dillon and cohort had been arrested in Tucson and would be there for some time. This was a great relief to them both. Will could live a normal life without always having to look over his shoulder. The first thing he did when he arrived at home was put his gun away. Then after a visit with his mother he went to find Ben.

School began a couple days later and Will settled into a routine that included study, work, and enjoying himself with his friends. Mrs. Dillon had started working part time for Helen Carter so Will was freed up to take a job working for Alf Helgerson at his blacksmith shop every day after school. The work was hard and hot but Will didn't mind at all. The heavy work hardened and added bulk to his arms and shoulders. He was growing up. He was tall for his age but not gangly. His chest and arms were muscular, giving him a strength and stamina uncommon in boys his age. His hair was sandy colored and, like his father, his steel blue eyes mirrored his feelings. They would twinkle with merriment, but they could also flash with anger and at times they seemed to penetrate deep into a person's soul. His physical bearing coupled with his warm and caring nature caused people to like and respect him.

His mother marveled at the mental and spiritual maturity he displayed, especially when he and Nathan became involved in one of their discussions; which seemed to be happening quite regularly. They had chosen her kitchen as their ideal location for these talks. She often joined them and soon learned that her views were welcomed and valued.

As time passed the discussions turned more personal in nature. Nathan talked of his past and in so doing exposed, not only his personal dreams and ambitions, but the scars and hurts that existed in his life. His youth had not been easy, with an abusive father and a mother who had deserted him when he was twelve years old. This had forced him to grow up fast and learn to survive in an all too often hostile world.

In return Helen related her story and that of Will. As they began to know each other better a mutual respect developed. There was also a comfort and sense of freedom that grew between the three.

Nathan was often required to be away, usually for only a short time, but there were some trips that involved several days or more. During these times the house seemed to be empty, missing something vital. Although there were boarders around they were not able to fill the void Nathan's absence created.

Indeed, there were subtle but definite changes taking place in the Carter household. Will began to notice he was no longer the center of attention. He also noticed an almost imperceptible change in his mother's demeanor. She spent just a little more time with her hair in the morning and her dress was always freshly ironed. Then there was the time he went to the cupboard for the left over piece of pie he knew was there, only to find it gone. He became a little irritated when his mother informed him that Nathan had looked like he needed something to "perk him up" so she had given it to him.

Not too long after the pie incident Will found himself ousted from his favorite chair. He was relaxing in it one evening when Nathan and his mother came into the living room. Looking at Will she said, "Why don't you let Nathan sit there? He's had a hard day and needs to relax." Will looked at her, dumbfounded. That was *his* chair. At least it had been his chair up until now. Somehow Will knew it was no longer the case. Standing to his feet he waved Nathan into the chair. Nathan gave Will an embarrassed smile and spread his hands as if to say 'it wasn't my idea,' and meekly sat down.

Suddenly things began to come together in Will's mind and the truth of the matter became clear. This was something Will had never considered before. Did he like it? He wasn't sure. He spent the next several days mulling the matter over, taking the question very seriously. After all, it was his mother's future he was deciding. Finally after careful consideration he made his decision, and he wasted no time making it known. Marching into the kitchen he fixed his gaze upon his surprised mother and said "Mom, regarding the matter of Nathan Penny...you have my approval." With that he turned and marched out leaving his mother staring dumbly at his retreating figure.

As the weeks turned into months, a bond grew between the three. From Will's point of view, Nathan had filled the hole left in his life when his father died. As he observed the interaction between Nathan and his mother, he recognized that spark of life that died with his father, returning and restoring the vibrancy that had made her such a beautiful woman. Once again her speech was punctuated with laughter and the mischievous sparkle returned to her eyes. Her sense of humor returned along with a sense of optimism. Once again she had a reason for getting out of bed each day, other than simply for the sake of her son. Her walk had the spring of anticipation in it.

Nathan had grown to love them both. He wondered if his desire for a wife and family would be granted, but he harbored a secret fear that refused to allow him to broach the subject. What if she turned him down? He couldn't bear the thought of losing what he now had. Better to be satisfied than take the risk of losing it all.

Will eventually grew exasperated at him. Couldn't he see what was taking place? Look at the way she dressed, and always made sure her hair was just right, and what about his favorite chair now belonging to Nathan. And who was it that always got the last piece of pie? It was all getting on Will's nerves and he finally decided to do something about it. So it was that he informed his friend it was time for a man to man talk.

"Come on Nathan, we're going down by the river." Helen smiled, somewhat puzzled and a little amused as she watched them walk down the lane. She couldn't hear but she saw the animated gestures of Will and the surprised look on Nathan's face as he turned to stare at him. "Nathan, you have got to be the most block headed, slow witted person I have ever known!"

Nathan was shocked and a little angry. "Hold on now son, Just what has you so all riled up?"

"Why, can't you see she's just waiting for you to ask her? Good grief, how much pie is she going to have to stuff down you before you get the message? That's supposed to be my pie and she's just wasting it on you."

Nathan was totally confused now; "What does pie have to do with anything?"

Will sputtered and stammered trying to collect himself. "Well if you can't figure that out you are hopeless and I give up."

With that Will stomped off leaving Nathan staring blankly at his retreating form. Suddenly Will turned around and shouted "You want to know what pie has to do with it, You just march yourself back to the kitchen and ask mom! She'll tell you what pie has to do with it!" Will stormed of into the darkness.

Helen had heard the last part of the conversation as Will's voice had become louder and louder. As a result by the time a totally dumfounded Nathan arrived back at the kitchen she was holding her sides, totally helpless with laughter. He just stared at her for a minute then the truth began to dawn on him. His face broke into a huge smile and he stepped towards her. She put her arms around him and stopped laughing long enough to kiss him then she dissolved again into laughter.

Helen was not the only one who had heard the exchange on the lane. Pastor Tomkins had been out for a walk and had heard it all. He had also been observing the two for some time and was not at all surprised. Stepping onto the porch he knocked softly.

Helen opened the door, wiping the tears from her eyes and trying to quell the laughter that wanted to break out.

When Will finally returned he found the three sitting at the table drinking coffee. Helen was forced to turn away for a moment while Nathan, straight faced said, "Will, your mother and I have something to ask you, would you consider granting me your mother's hand in marriage?" With that the three adults broke out in laughter again. Will stared at them for a moment then he rushed over, shook Nathan's hand and hugged his mother. Looking at Pastor Tompkins he asked, "How did you get here so fast?" Once again the room erupted with laughter.

With wedding plans and decisions to make, Helen and Nathan had less time for Will. This freed him up to spend more time with Ben, Wayne, and Running Bird. Wayne and Running Bird were slowly becoming friends, simply because Will gave them no choice, insisting that each person in the foursome was important to the others. As a result a strong sense of loyalty began to develop, Though none of them realized it now the bond of loyalty they were building would help them through a time of crisis when they had to depend upon each other for their very lives.

Time brings changes and Will and his friends were changing as they matured. Wayne was concerned for his mother and was taking on more responsibility. He was also experiencing conflict with his older brothers because of his loyalty to Running Bird and Will. Ben was doing well in school and making plans to study in the East when he finished high school. He had gone to an eye specialist in San Diego and was fitted with glasses. For the first time in his life he could focus and read without extreme effort. Now he had hopes of becoming an eye specialist and doing research on the connection between eye problems and one's ability to read with understanding. This was an idea very few people gave any credit to and Ben was determined to help others with his problem if at all possible.

Running Bird was becoming restless, trying to cope with a growing inner struggle. Only Will knew of the turmoil he was hiding within himself and he felt helpless to do anything but wait until his friend was ready to share his heart with him. The opportunity came one warm afternoon; One of those days when the swimming hole was the only place a boy wanted to be. Both Ben and Wayne were busy so that left Will and Running Bird alone.

As they sat on the sandy bank Running Bird absently threw little twigs and pebbles into the water. He was unusually quiet and Will was hesitant to break into his friends thoughts. Suddenly Running Bird blurted out "White men speak with a double tongue."

"What do you mean?' asked Will.

"Your preacher says God loves every one the same. He says we are to love everyone the same. White people sing about God and talk about God but they cheat the Indians and mistreat the Mexicans."

Once the words began to flow there was no stopping Running Bird. "When an Indian seeks the White man's Jesus, he is told he must change his way of living. He must cut his hair and put on White mans clothes. He is told he must turn his back on the old customs and his people's way of life. He must call the Creator by the White man's name. It costs the Indian everything."

Will listened quietly as Running Bird continued. "When the white man seeks Jesus, he prays and goes into the water. He gives up nothing. He still treats the Indian bad; I can feel the mocking eyes on me. I have heard the words of the people in father's store. There is no place for me in the white man's world. You and Ben are my only friends."

Will sat silent for some time vainly seeking to form an argument that would convince his friend, but deep inside he knew Running Bird was all too right in much of what he had said. He desperately searched for words to explain the contradictions that discredited the teachings of Christianity. Not that they were wrong but rather the actions of men made them seem a lie. But how could he reassure his friend and make him see that there was a place for him? Will walked home with a heavy heart. He also determined to do all he could to make things fair for every person regardless of his race.

The days and weeks flew by and Will's world revolved around the planning and preparation for his mother's wedding. Nathan and Will wanted a small private ceremony but Helen had other ideas. With the reinforcement of the other women of her social circle the men were forced to capitulate and plans went forward for a ceremony and reception that would qualify as one of the important events on Yuma's social calendar. The community would have been surprised had it known of the plans being made by another group; Plans that when carried out would throw the town into turmoil.

⤜ ⤛

Mean while the coming wedding was having it's effect on the principal participants. Helen was becoming more serene each day. She and Clara Dillon were spending a lot of time in Helen's room, working on her wedding dress. They were also becoming close friends. Clara willingly joined in with Helen's excitement while

Helen, ever sensitive, provided encouragement and support to Clara as she struggled with her failing marriage.

Nathan seemed to be loosing ground, becoming more agitated as the wedding day approached. He finally went to see Pastor Tomkins who reassured him he would be a good husband. This helped but Nathan secretly dreaded the day itself, convinced he would spoil the ceremony.

Will was becoming a tyrant, constantly reminding Nathan of tasks that should be attended to and things he should beware of. His greatest concern was that Nathan would blow his lines during the ceremony and he reminded him of it almost daily. Nathan began to wonder if it had been wise to ask Will to be his best man.

The day finally arrived. Will woke with a start and his mind immediately filled with details to worry about and instructions for everyone. Helen was still calm and relaxed but Nathan was a bundle of nerves. He was also fed up with Will. Helen wisely gave instructions to Clara Dillon that Will and Nathan keep away from each other until it was time to meet with the Pastor.

The hours seemed to drag. Would the appointed time never come? When Will and Nathan finally arrived at the church they found it packed to overflowing. This was almost too much for Nathan. Seeing a horse tied at the hitching rail he said "Maybe I'll just get on that horse and ride out of here."

"Maybe I'll just tie you up along with the horse," Will retorted. They stood looking at each other for several seconds then they both began to laugh. "Lets go find the preacher and get this over with." As if responding to Nathan's statement Pastor Tomkins walked around the corner and it was no time before preacher, groom and best man stood in their places waiting for the bride.

Nathan's nervousness left him momentarily while Helen walked down the isle. He was totally consumed with her as she smiled into his eyes, and felt that his life was really just beginning as she took her place beside him. A nudge from Will broke the spell and Pastor Tomkins began the ceremony.

Once again Nathan began to perspire as the time for the vows drew near. He wondered if his voice would fail him altogether. Suddenly the question was put before him. All that was required was "I Do." He looked into Helen's eyes and opened his mouth just as Will's elbow found its mark in his ribs. Out came "Ouch! I Do!

.. Dog gone it Will!" There was a slight stirring in the congregation as Helen gave Will a withering glare then turned to reassure Nathan with a smile.

Will produced the ring right on cue and after a brief explanation of it's significance, which went over Nathan's head, Nathan was instructed to repeat after the Pastor "With this ring I thee wed." Pastor Tomkin's voice was confidant and Nathan was determined his would be also. With his voice clear and strong he announced "Wit dis wing I dee wed." Helen sucked in her breath as she looked wide-eyed at Nathan, who couldn't believe what he had just said. An awestruck quietness settled over congregation. It was as though even the church mice stopped to acknowledge the all time best blunder.

The rest of the ceremony was a blur for Nathan and he was grateful when it was all over. He found little relief, as he and Helen wondered amongst the guests following the reception. Unfortunately the standard comment for this event brought the discomfort back; "It was a lovely ceremony."

After the guests had gone Will helped Nathan pack the buckboard. He couldn't resist the temptation to tease his new step-father. "By the way Nathan, just what does 'Wit dis wing I Dee wed' mean?"

"It means Will, that if I ever hear that phrase again from you I'm going to knock you in the head." That sounded reasonable to Will under the circumstances, and he willingly helped his mom with her luggage. In no time they were ready to leave. As they drove away Will sent a short prayer of thanksgiving and also asked for protection for the two most precious people in his life.

As he went to sleep that night he was unaware of the next adventure that he would experience. The trouble began just a few days after the marriage of Helen and Nathan. While they were away on their honeymoon Mrs. Dillon and Wayne moved in so she could manage the boarding house. It was during this time that Myron Hamilton was kidnapped. He was the ten-year old son of Thomas Hamilton, who was considered to be the wealthiest man in the territory. A ransom note was delivered demanding fifty thousand dollars within a week or the boy would be killed.

All efforts to find him and the kidnappers had been fruitless and the deadline was only two days away. The common consensus was that even if the money was delivered the boy would never be seen again. This was based on an almost identical case that took place in Phoenix a few months earlier, where the money was paid and the victim was found several weeks later having been dead for some time.

Will had found it almost impossible to sleep for several nights so the tap on his window brought an immediate response. He opened the window and Running Bird fell into the room with a thud.

"We found him, Will." Will didn't have to ask who.

"Where is he? How did you find him?" Running bird explained that Wayne had spotted an old associate of his dad named Murphy. He followed him and heard him and another man talking. They were in town to get supplies, and after a few drinks they headed back to their hideout. Wayne followed them counting on his friends to find his trail and help him free the boy.

Will wanted to notify the sheriff but Running Bird pointed out that he was out of town and trying to raise a posse would be futile and would waste time. Will instructed Running Bird to get Ben, then after filling a sack with food he went to the barn to saddle the two horses Nathan owned. Ben and Running Bird soon arrived and the three were on their way. Will prayed that they would be able to find the trail Wayne was leaving, and that they could come up with a way to set Myron free.

Fortunately it was a moonlit night and Running Bird had no trouble finding the trail. They were able to travel fast and by the time the sun was up they had caught up with Wayne, who knew the exact location of the outlaws. Wayne pointed out a coulee that led down to the river. The coulee, caused by years of erosion as the water of many rains rushed back to the Colorado River, was several feet deep and about three hundred feet long. About a hundred feet from the river it took a bend. On this bend was a stone cabin with a stone shed some twenty feet behind it. The cabin was situated so that it was impossible to approach from any direction without being seen. Wayne was convinced Myron was being held in the shed.

They had three problems to solve. First they would have to steal the horses or they would never make the twenty miles back to town before being overtaken. Then they would have to free Myron. These were relatively easy. The big problem was how to deal with the four outlaws. Will had his gun but a fight was not an option. Somehow they had to get the outlaws down to the river so they could make their escape without being seen. There had to be a way. Crawling through the brush they found a spot where they could look down and see the cabin and shed. They located the horses by pin-pointing the sound of their stomping and blowing, and they discovered that there was always at least one man on guard. He spent most of his time on the cabin porch but he periodically walked back to the shed to check the prisoner.

Will was in no hurry. Whatever they did would have to be done after dark. Fortunately there was enough brush to provide added cover, but they would have to be careful not to make any noise for if the outlaws became aware of their presence they would have no chance against them. The rest of the day was spent in resting, and observing the routine of the four men. By dusk Will had formulated a plan and calling the others he laid it out. Each one had his part, and each part was vital to the success of the others.

Once again they were forced to wait. They could do nothing until an hour before dawn, then each part of the plan must be carried out like clockwork. Will went over each ones task again as he whittled on a piece of wood and separated a cord from a coil of rope. After what seemed like an eternity the banter of the outlaws ceased. They had spent most of the evening arguing about what to do with Myron. That they fully expected to receive the ransom was obvious. That they had no intention of releasing him was also plain.

Murphy wanted to kill him now but was over ruled. He was still more valuable alive as a bargaining piece. The rest of the discussion was over the most entertaining way to do it when the time came, and what they were going to do with the ransom money.

Will and his friends were filled with revulsion at the savage cruelty these men displayed. They also understood that if they were caught they would also die. Like soldiers waiting for the coming battle, each one became lost in their own thoughts. Will struggled with a sense of guilt. It was foolish to go against these seasoned men and he felt responsible for the safety of his friends. Yet he knew they were the only chance Myron had. They were able to get some sleep as the night dragged on but they were far from rested when Will announced it was time. Never the less it was with relief that they set out, each to his own task.

Will headed back to a grove of trees some five hundred feet from the mouth of the coulee. There he approached a huge hornet's nest he had spotted the day before. Working quickly he stuffed the plug, he had whittled, into the opening, then he cut the nest loose and headed back toward the cabin. He was careful to keep from shaking his cargo.

Running Bird and Wayne carefully made their way to where the horses were tied, keeping themselves in the darkest shadows. Working quickly but quietly they gave them some grain to keep them calm and soon had them saddled. Ben was stationed at the shed and by whispering through a knothole, had alerted Myron to what they were doing.

Now it was up to the guard. He must be drawn to the shed without those sleeping in the cabin being alerted. Soon the sun came up. When it's rays got around to the porch Will gave a short whistle. At Ben's word Myron began pounding on the door. Startled, the man on guard jumped from the porch and ran to the shed. As soon as he was out of sight Will sprinted for the cabin, praying that those inside were asleep. Reaching the porch he quickly tied the cord, he had made the night before, onto the plug on the hornet's nest. Then he dropped it on the floor and ran. He could hear the angry hornets vainly trying to escape.

Will concealed himself in some brush opposite the cabin and waited for the guard to return. He didn't have long to wait, and as soon as he stepped up on the porch Will gave the cord a jerk. As luck would have it the cabin door opened just as the hornets began to pour out of the nest. The three men walked through the door and joined the guard in a swarm of angry hornets. Then Pandemonium reigned as the men, shouting and cursing, vainly tried to fight the hornets off. Finally one of them yelled, "Head for the river!" and off they went, arms flailing and legs thrashing, racing for the protection the river would provide.

They were so occupied with the hornets that they didn't notice the boys yank the door from the shed and free Myron. Each time one of them poked his head out of the water for air several hornets would deliver a painful sting. The boys were soon mounted, and running their horses up the Coulee they made their escape. They stopped long enough to retrieve Nathan's horses. This gave them each a horse with two to spare, and they knew they would not be overtaken.

As the reality of their success hit them they began to laugh and whoop and wave their hats in the air. The stress and pent up energy gave way to shear joy as they laughed at the sight of the angry outlaws jumping and flailing their way down to the river. After a few minutes they slowed their horses to a trot.

It was some time before the hornets settled down and allowed the men to venture out of the water. When they discovered the cord and plug beside the hornets nest and found the horses and hostage missing, they were filled with rage. They also felt humiliated and vowed to get revenge. Then the seriousness of their situation began to sink in. They had to get away before the law came looking for them. They decided to head for Picacho, only a few miles distant. There they would replace their horses and after laying low for a while they would head for Tucson.

By the time the five boys arrived at the Hamilton place they were exhausted. Mrs. Hamilton was sitting on the veranda and spotted them coming when they were still some distance away. She assumed they were just some cowhands or part of the posse returning and didn't look again until they were quite near. When she did recognize Myron she gave a yell and ran into the house screaming for her husband. Not finding him, she turned around and ran across the yard to meet her son. In her exuberance she reached up and pulled Myron out of the saddle and they both fell onto the ground.

Soon Mr. Hamilton and some others, including Pastor Tomkins, arrived. They all started talking at once, asking what had happened and how they had been able to set Myron free. With all the commotion and distraction, and being exhausted as they were, they were not able to fill in all of the details until the next day. Soon the whole town had heard the story.

The boys were instant heroes and were each presented with five hundred dollars, which was put in trust for them until their eighteenth birthday. Their story was also featured in all the major newspapers in Arizona and Southern California.

Once again life took on a routine. For Will it included work and school. He also took a few trips with Nathan. Will was maturing. No longer a boy, he took on more and more, the aspect and bearing of a man. While concerned that Will had made some enemies Nathan was confident that he would be able to hold his own against them when and if the need came.

Will loved the times he spent in the desert. He had learned much from Nathan, both about the desert and himself, and about human nature. His love and respect for Nathan as a friend and a father had deepened

To Will the desert presented a picture of life. It held a uniqueness of it's own, Embodying beauty, mystery, and promise, yet ever fraught with danger. It seemed to beckon one to seek out it's treasures, luring many an unfortunate wanderer just a little beyond the point his limits and resources would allow him to go. Drawn by a silent promise of wealth or adventure, he would find himself trapped by his own greed and carelessness. Then the other nature of the desert would be revealed; harsh, without mercy, sometimes hateful, it would attack with a sand storm or deceive and taunt by a mirage, causing the traveler to spend all his strength and energy, and eventually sucking the life out of the unfortunate victim.

Yet once in a while one would be spared from his doom. Was it a miracle or pure luck that led him to an unknown water hole or that brought another traveler across his path? Yet so often the one so fortunately saved, would return only to repeat his mistake.

There was yet another aspect of the desert that fascinated Will. While having a beauty all it's own it never the less seemed jaded as if by some past curse, or some mysterious secret. Where life had once thrived it now seemed oppressed by the heavy arm of death. Will begin to think of it as the law of the desert. Within this law something vital was missing and Will understood it. Regardless of what beauty or potential it promised, the desert could not deliver. Without water it would remain parched and capricious, dealing disappointment and death to many an unwary traveler. Similarly, many a man had invested himself in the pursuits of life only to have his soul sucked dry of all it possessed, leaving only a withered and shrunken shell. A good example of this was Crazy Tom Pound.

Will could not look into the desert without remembering the story of the Israelites who had followed Moses into the wilderness. Finding themselves thirsty and without water they cried out to God, who in response instructed Moses to strike a rock. Out flowed life-giving water. Later in history another man walked the barren path in another desert, and talked of mans spiritual thirst. The rock Moses struck was a picture of Jesus who alone could quench man's thirst. So often men sought to quench their thirst with that which couldn't fulfil, and neglected the one that offered living water. But the Galilean had said "come to me and I will give you living water."

Will was learning more and more that the world was filled with springs and treasures that could not bring satisfaction. He needed to beware of the subtle counterfeits and stay fixed on his purpose. He wondered what the Master Planner had in store for him and entered his fifteenth year, alive with anticipation and determination to realize his destiny wherever providence led.

Chapter 5

S HE SAT LIKE a stone oblivious to the rain that had drenched her to the bone, and unaware of the passage of time. She didn't feel the dark chill creeping over her as the sun, as if fleeing the scene, hid itself behind the trees. She saw only the two graves before her and read again the name of her father, Thomas Sutter, Born Aug. 2, 1836-Died Mar. 23, 1873. A sob caught in her throat as her eyes fell on the other grave. It had no name or date. In fact the ground had not yet settled. It was too recent; for her mother had been in her grave only two hours.

A black cloud of despair and loneliness enveloped her, ripping at her soul, as she once again gave way to the tears that demanded release. She was barely aware of the footsteps that approached or the strained voice that called her. "Becky Ann Sutter, you're going to catch your death. You come home now and get into some warm clothes." Forced to tear herself from the protective shroud of solitude, without a word Becky took the hand extended by her Aunt Martha and allowed herself to be led through the trees to the little farm nestled in the forest of Northwest Washington. She wondered if she would ever be free of the overwhelming pain that threatened to crush her.

Time is said to be a healer but to Becky healing seemed to be slow in coming. She was strong in spirit though, and as the days dragged into months she kept fighting the relentless emptiness and grief that lurked in the corners of her world, and ever threatened to devour any peace or joy that sought lodging within her. Coupled with her loneliness was a nagging sense of guilt caused by the feeling that she was a burden to her uncle and aunt. Her parents had provided a moderate inheritance, which had been put in trust until her eighteenth birthday. She knew her uncle made barely enough to get by on and felt she was just an added mouth to feed. She did all she could to help with the farm and with housework but could not rid herself of the persistent conviction that she was a burden too heavy for her aunt and uncle to bear. If only she could take some of her money and give it to them. She had tried but access was denied.

There was more involved than the money issue alone. Becky sensed that while her aunt and uncle loved her and wished the best for her, they were not able to open their hearts completely to her as one would their own daughter. She felt like a guest in their home, welcome as long as she needed to be there but expected to find her own way, as soon she was able. That would free them from an obligation put upon them by the death of her mother.

Becky had one friend in whom she could confide, Dr. Wilbur Cully. He had spent hours with her father when he was dying; and again with her mother, he went far beyond the call of duty. What was so remarkable was the fact that at sixty-eight years of age he was retired and was motivated by compassion alone.

Becky always felt welcome at his home, and had a freedom to open her heart, sensing genuine interest in what happened to her. For this reason she was open to his advice and ready to consider an idea he posed to her.   Dr. Cully had practiced medicine in Yuma until his retirement when he moved to Seattle to be with his daughter. Now he was ready to return to the warm, dry climate of the desert and his daughter had agreed to accompany him. He was not able to care for Becky himself but he thought he knew of someone who could. With Becky's consent he wrote a letter to Helen Carter suggesting an arrangement that would be beneficial to both her and Becky. Becky could work for her room and board and a small wage. This would provide a place of security and stability for her, and give Helen some much-needed relief from her heavy workload.

When Helen received the letter she shared it at once with Nathan and Will. Both agreed that it was a good idea, which would fit well into their current plans. Yuma was growing and with it the need for living facilities such as Helen's boarding house provided. This presented an opportunity for Nathan and Helen to work together and enable Nathan to quit his job, which required his absence from home more than he liked, and which exposed him to danger. He wanted to enjoy his new family with no interruptions.

They had already drawn up the plans for an addition of eight more rooms. Nathan had withdrawn his savings to finance the project and he and Will would do the bulk of the work. Helen wasted no time getting an answer back to the doctor, being careful to inform him of her marriage and resulting name change. She also enclosed a letter to Becky assuring her that she would be welcome and would no doubt fit right into the family.

The mail traveled slowly and by the time plans were finalized and preparations completed several months had gone by. Becky's loneliness had slowly given place to anticipation as she exchanged letters with Helen. She had been told so much about Will and Nathan she could hardly wait to meet them. She felt like she already knew Helen, sensing a compassion and love that her aunt Martha had been unable to provide. So it was with excitement that she received the departure date from Dr. Cully

Interestingly it was a year, to the day, of her mother's death.

The days flew by, filled with packing and saying farewell to her friends. Then, suddenly it was the evening before she was to leave and she had only one task left to perform. She must say farewell to her parents. She approached the gravesite reverently and sat quietly between the headstones as if listening for a word of encouragement or instruction.

After several minutes of silence, memories began to instill themselves into her thoughts. She began to relive the days before her father took sick and was soon laughing as forgotten memories were called to her mind. Her mood became warm then tender as the words of her parents came back to her, so clear that it could have been this day that they had been spoken. It was as if her parents were sitting in the little glen with her.   Becky completely lost track of time as she once again heard the laughter of her father and the music of her mother's voice as she sang the old hymns she loved so well. She felt again the love and unity that had flowed between them as they sat hands and hearts joined in prayer. The ecstasy of oblivion that cradled her began to crumble as the sound of a small animal scampering through the brush demanded her return to reality. It was with a mild shock that she found herself alone, looking again at the headstones of her mother and father.

The spell was broken and she knew she must pull herself away. The tears came as she realized she might never stand on this ground again; ground she considered sacred. Not wanting anyone to intrude upon her final moments with her parents, she knelt briefly and prayed for wisdom and strength to fulfil the wishes she imagined her parents held for her. Then with a barely audible goodbye she put her hand briefly on each headstone, and turning from them, she fled.

The next day the sky was clear and the air crisp. It was six o'clock in the morning and Becky felt like she hadn't slept at all the night before. She looked in awe at the ship they would spend several days on. They were to sail down the coast and all the way around the Baja peninsula, then up the Gulf of California to Port Isabel. There they would get a riverboat the rest of the way to Yuma. She looked forward to the adventure but anticipated meeting her new family with excitement tempered a little by fear.

Will and Nathan were very busy with the building of the addition. Will had time for little other than school and work. It was also a happy time. He was learning, and with the increase in skill was a general growth and maturing. His sixteenth birthday came and went but he possessed the size and strength of a mature man. He also loved his home where he felt secure in an environment of love and respect.

He had all but forgotten the scrapes he had with the Dillon's and as time went by his caution was replaced by a carefree, if not a careless spirit.

Things seemed to be going well, almost too well. Will still had enemies who resented him and would use any means to get back at him. One such person was Wade Dillon. Will had frustrated Wade's plans as well as those of his father and brother and had also befriended Wayne. If anything, Wade was worse than his father, full of hate and desperately wanting to draw Will into a fight. If he hurt a friend of Will's so much the better. Wade saw his chance late one afternoon.

Will was working at the blacksmith shop during a lull in the construction at home and Ben had stopped by to visit. Along with the small talk was a warning from Ben that Wade was back in town and doing some pretty loose talking about what he was going to do to Will.

Ben left and headed down the street unaware that Wade was watching him.

"Hey cross-eyes, what are you doing in the man's part of town?" Ben tensed up but kept walking while reaching down to calm Happy who had responded with a low growl.

"Hey Ben, I think the only thing on earth uglier than you is that mangy Mutt and I think I'll take care of that." Suddenly a shot rang out followed by a cry of agony from Happy. Ben stood paralyzed by shock, not able to comprehend what had just happened.

As reality hit him he knelt down and cradled Happy's head in his hands. Happy looked briefly at Ben then his eyes clouded in death. Ben was helpless to do anything but sit beside his dog and sob in his grief. Those who had seen it turned in disbelief and stared at Wade, who was taken back a little by the scorn he saw on their faces. He quickly regained his haughty demeanor though as he waited Will's arrival.

Meanwhile Will had heard the shot and hurried to his friend. He sat beside him, arm around his shoulder not ashamed of the tears he was shedding. Will sat for some time, his brain refusing to make sense of what had happened. Then he began to regain his focus as the sound of Wades voice began to intrude into his consciousness. "Well, look at who's crying, and over a good-for-nothing mongrel."

Will began to tremble with rage and he knew he must control himself. "Come on Ben, lets take care of Happy." Picking up the dog he walked back up the street until he came to a large tree. There he buried his friend's dog then he took him home. Ben rushed past his mother, into his room and once more gave vent to his grief.

As Will walked back towards town he asked God to take the murder from his heart. He knew he couldn't remove it himself. He also knew he was going to deal with Wade Dillon and he was going to do it now. It didn't matter that Wade was six years older and twenty pounds heavier.

By the time Will got back, Wade was alone. No one wanted to have anything to do with him, or have it appear they were connected with him in any way. Will did not utter a word, he just walked straight for Wade, his eyes piercing those of Wade.

"What are you looking at?" No answer came from Will. He just kept coming. Wade began to sweat and looked away seeking to break free of Will's gaze but was forced to look back. He saw that Will was not wearing a gun. This made him all the more fearful. "I said what are you looking at?" There was an edge of panic in his voice, and he began to backtrack, but his retreat was stopped by the barber shop wall.

Will quickly covered the last few feet. When within reach his right hand shot out and grabbed Wade by the throat. Putting all his strength into his legs he lifted him off his feet, and slammed him against the wall where he remained suspended. Wades right hand fumbled for his gun but Will was too quick. His left hand had already removed it and tossed it into a nearby horse trough.

Wades eyes bulged out as his feet kicked, frantically seeking solid footing. For all practical purposes he was being hung.

"What am I looking at?" Will shouted "I'm looking at a coward!" He held him until his eyes rolled back in his head and his tongue began to hang out, then he let him fall.

Will looked at those who were standing around but saw no hostility. There were expressions of shock at the speed and strength Will had demonstrated as well as respect. They all wondered what Will would do next. They didn't have long to wait.

Will stripped Wade of his gun belt and hung it over the pommel of his saddle then taking a coil of rope he tied Wades hands together. After fishing his gun out of the trough he waited for him to regain consciousness. Wade began to stir and soon was able to stand though he was unsteady. Will mounted the horse and wrapping the rope around the pommel began pulling Wade up the street. "Come on Wade, your taking your last walk up this street." Wade blanched in fear but had no choice other than to be dragged by the horse.

Will stopped at the blacksmith shop long enough to fill a large canteen then continued on until he came to the road leading North East out of town. "You're going to get on your horse and you're not going to stop until you get to Gila Bend, and you're never coming back here. If you do you will be very sorry."

"What about my gun?" stammered Wade.

"I'll let Ben decide that." With that Will put him on the horse and sent him on his way, then he turned and headed for Ben's house.

News of the incident spread fast. There was a general feeling of respect for Will and genuine sorrow for Ben. Though he was just a stray dog people understood the attachment between Happy and Ben. They also knew there was bad blood between Will and the Dillon's. It would only be a matter of time before violence would erupt. One thing people did not realize was the speed and accuracy with which Will handled a gun. That was a secret Will determined to keep to himself. He also determined not to take a life. From that time on he began carrying his gun knowing the next time he met a Dillon he would face more than one.

Chapter 6

T HE LONG AWAITED day finally arrived. Becky stood on the dock looking expectantly for someone resembling the description Dr. Cully had given of Helen Carter. The journey from Seattle had stretched from one of weeks into that of months when Dr. Cully suffered an infected appendix and they were forced to stay in San Diego while he fought his life and death battle.

It was a bad time for Becky as she seemed to be reliving the deathwatch over her own parents. Never the less she faithfully remained at the man's bedside. She and Rose, the Doctor's daughter shared a journey through the depths of despair to the heights of hope and back again as his condition fluctuated several times. In the end he miraculously began a slow but steady process of healing that took several weeks. Now they were at the end of their journey and Becky had only one thing in mind; get Dr. Cully settled in a comfortable bed.

Becky took in the scene around her. The muddy Colorado river was anything but peaceful as it churned, and rumbled, and roared its deep throated and boastful tale of passage through Colorado, Utah, and New Mexico. Then as if assuming some divinely appointed authority it continued on, carving the boarder between Arizona and

Nevada, then California and Arizona before spending itself in the Gulf of California.

It seemed to claim credit as a building and shaping force without which the nation could not reach it's potential. After all was it not present at the birth of the Grand Canyon? Did it not provide transportation and irrigation over a distance of fourteen hundred miles, benefiting thousands of people?

Becky was unaware of the river's boasts as she studied the bleached soil and barren mountains that bore no resemblance to the lush green hills and forests of the home she had left behind. Though she was conscious of the heat, there was never the less a softness to the atmosphere that she found comforting and she marveled that she could see for miles in the clear sun-cleansed air.

It wasn't long before Becky saw an approaching wagon. She recognized Helen Carter at once. Then her eyes fell on Will. At the sight of him her heart gave a little leap and her breath caught in her throat. She was somewhat surprised and irritated as she felt her face flush. She had never reacted this way before and she didn't like it one bit. With some effort she regained her composure as Helen walked toward her and welcomed her with an embrace.

Becky was relieved when Nathan appeared and the formality of introductions gave way to the task of getting the Doctor and the traveler's luggage loaded onto the wagon. She found herself unable to resist the occasional glance at Will, and found his behavior quite amusing. She began to wonder if his mother had neglected to include everything about him in her letters. He seemed to have some kind of problem.

He apparently had a speech problem as all he was able to do was mutter a couple of unintelligible noises that made no sense when introduced to her. Then he promptly walked face first into one of the horses and apologized to the horse, an action that was not lost on Nathan. For some reason he kept taking his hat off and putting it back on, each time running his hand around the sweat band trying to get rid of the perspiration that was flowing freely off his head.

The ride from the ferry landing to the Carter home was quiet except for the occasional comment of Helen and the sporadic laughter of Nathan. Each outburst was quelled by a stern and meaningful look from Helen. Nathan was finding Will's behavior quite amusing to say the least. No sooner would he get his mirth under control when he would get another glimpse of Will's tortured face, or Will would say or do something totally out of keeping with the situation. Then he would succumb once again to laughter.

Finally in exasperation Helen told him to mount his horse and ride on ahead. She gave the reins to Will who flicked one of the horses on the back and said, "let's go Sweetheart." With that Nathan burst into laughter and put his horse to a run. Helen stared at Will "What did you call the horse?" she asked in disbelief.

Will, red faced was unable to answer. Becky sat in the back with her face averted, seeking to hide the redness of her cheeks, while Wilber and Rose Cully restrained themselves, sharing a knowing smile. Helen could only mutter that she didn't know what in the world had gotten control of Nathan. So it was that Becky Ann Sutter was introduced to her new family.

The evening meal was torment for both Becky and Will. Helen innocently placed them next to each other at the table and both of them were experiencing feelings that were at the same time pleasant and excruciating. Will was still tongue tied and awkward, afraid to attempt anything. Things began to go wrong when, for no reason, his fork jumped from his hand, turning a summersault and rattling off his plate and finally landing next to Becky's foot. He had no difficulty reaching down to retrieve it except that in so doing, his head briefly came to rest on Becky's shoulder.

Helen didn't notice him drop the fork but she did see his head on Becky's shoulder. Her reaction was swift and decicieve. A well placed kick under the table and a glare of ice had its effect on her son, or so she thought. No sooner had he regained his composure then the troublesome fork once again wrenched itself free of his grasp and clattered to the floor. This time he mumbled a swear word, much to his mothers shock and embarrassment, and proceeded to finish his meal with a spoon. Becky was experiencing a shyness she had never before experienced, and was fighting sudden urges to giggle. This was tempered with a feeling of compassion and warmth toward Will.

Rose and Dr. Cully were exchanging amused glances and Helen Carter was red faced and dumbfounded. Nathan was enjoying himself immensely. Along with his embarrassment Will was furious with Nathan, who was taking every opportunity to insert a jibe at him. Finally Nathan leaned back, and stretching his arms over his head said, "Well I guess its chore time; do you want to help me feed Diamond and Sweetheart Will?"

Will lurched to his feet, stumbled out the back door, and made for the sanctuary of the barn, followed closely by Nathan who was once again in the throes of uncontrolled laughter.

This was too much for Will.

With a yell of rage he hurled himself at Nathan, who began back peddling to avoid the onrushing youth. Unfortunately his feet became tangled and he landed on his back in the straw. Nathan could do nothing helpless with laughter, as Will sprawled on top of him. In his exasperation Will grabbed a handful of straw and proceeded to stuff it into Nathan's mouth. As Nathan choked and sputtered Will said "I'm going to knock your head clean off if you don't keep quiet."

Suddenly a hand reached out of nowhere and taking Will's collar gently but firmly pulled him off the still helpless Nathan. Helen looked at both of them in total puzzlement. "What in the world is wrong with you two? Have you completely gone crazy? And what's this about Sweetheart?"

Nathan had purchased two horses to pull his wagon, for hauling building materials and needed supplies for the boarding house. Because of the markings on their foreheads they had the names of Star and Diamond.

Nathan, finally in control of himself, looked at Helen and said, "From now on Star goes by the name of Sweetheart and nobody is to know otherwise." Looking at Will, Nathan smiled and said, "Sorry I made it so rough on you Will but I just couldn't help it. I've never seen anyone so love sick in my life." Will's anger began to melt as he saw through the teasing of Nathan and sensed respect and affection.

"That's alright," answered Will, "And thanks about Star...I mean Sweetheart." With that Nathan and Will turned and walked away.

Helen watched them, shaking her head and chuckling. Every so often Nathan would make a comment to which Will responded with a good natured poke or shove. Helen was filled with gratitude as she watched the two men in her life. She felt a sense of security knowing they would never let anything happen to her. She knew the loyalty she saw between them extended to her also. She determined that

Becky Ann would be a full-fledged member of her home and family and experience the same sense of security and loyalty. The thought of Becky made her smile again. Helen had never seen Will act like this before. Love sometimes does strange things to young people and she wondered where it might lead her son.

The next day Will took Becky to school with him. There were only a couple of weeks remaining in the term but it was agreed Becky would get a better start next Fall if she broke the ice and got to know the other students now. As they walked, Will told her about some of the girls her age and what Miss Love was like. The awkwardness of the day before melted away as they became lost in their own little world. Will felt a warmness engulfing him as he answered her questions, and she began to talk about herself.

She described her former home and the emptiness she had felt when she lost her parents. She talked about the sea journey down the coast and how anxious she had been to meet him. Suddenly the talk ceased as they were reminded of the day before. Will began to blush and Becky smiled up at him. It was then that they noticed they were holding hands. They had been walking that way for some time but it had been so natural that neither had noticed when she had reached out and taken his hand. Now neither one made any attempt to separate. Instead they continued to walk, lost in their own thoughts, and letting the magic of this special moment wash over their beings.

As they walked Will was aware of the purposeful stride of Becky and the firm grip with which she held his hand. He had already taken note of her long blond hair and large blue eyes. It was those eyes that had rendered him totally helpless the day before. A sideward glance at the five foot four inch girl, who just happened to smile up at him, confirmed what he had already suspected; he had found his life partner.

With a start Will noticed the school yard before them as the little hand slipped from his. Becky hesitated as she scanned the faces of the students. Some were warm and friendly. Others were indifferent; and a few were openly hostile. At that moment Will appointed himself guardian and protector of the girl who in just a few short hours had changed his whole life and won his heart completely. It was a commitment that would not be without cost to him, but one that he would never go back on.

The day passed innocently enough except that Todd Dillon was busy planning. He was also recruiting some of the rougher members of the student body to join in his dirty scheme. In the end he was only able to enlist the Duffy boys. They were big and not too smart and they loved to fight. These were all traits that suited Todd's purposes very well. After school Will and Becky began walking up the path toward home, unaware that Todd and the Duffy boys were waiting in a secluded spot for their arrival.

Will and Becky were deep in conversation and didn't notice Todd until he stepped out of the brush and blocked their way. Tom and Bob Duffy quietly walked up behind Will and Becky. "Well if it isn't Will and his little kitten. Let's see if we can make her purr."

With that Tom grabbed Will from behind, pinning his arms at his sides, and Bob reached for Becky as Todd landed a couple heavy blows to Will's face. Becky was immediately enraged and being somewhat quicker than Bob expected, she side stepped and pushed on his shoulder as he lunged for her. This put her behind him and at a temporary advantage. Before he could react she jumped on his back and reaching around, dug a finger into each of his eyes.

Bob let out a cry of pain and fell to the ground where he lay clutching at his eyes. His cries were so terrible that both Todd and Tom stopped to see what had happened. This gave Will the chance he needed and breaking the grip of Tom he flew into Todd with a fury. The speed and power with which Will landed blow after blow soon rendered Todd helpless and it was only the presence of Tom that saved him from a severe beating.

Tom's immediate concern had been for his brother. After bending over him for a moment he remembered Will and looked up just in time to get a fist on the side of his head. He was unaware of what happened after that.

Will stood shaking, fighting the urge to deliver a couple of well placed kicks but he was no coward and wouldn't lower him self to that. He became aware of Bob's moans and then he heard the sobs of Becky. He instinctively reached for her and put his arm around her. They stood several minutes with Becky weeping on his shoulder. Finally she looked up at Will. "I was so frightened that they would hurt you. I don't understand how it can be; I've only known you for a day, but it's as if I've known you all my life. I've never felt like this before."

Will stood before her, his eyes moist with emotion, "Becky, I feel the same way. God has brought us together and I'll never let anyone hurt you." A pledge was made that moment in the hearts of a boy of sixteen and a girl barely fifteen. A pledge every bit as mature as if they were twice their ages.

Looking down at the three attackers, who were just now returning to the land of consciousness, Will gave an ironic little chuckle and said, "Well my little kitten I guess they found out what a wildcat you can be!" With that they turned and walked away leaving the three beaten youths sitting in the dust.

From that day on Will and Becky were inseparable. She became his best friend and he was her champion. During the last two weeks of school the older boys learned to treat her with respect. To do anything less was to invite the chastisement of Will and no one had any desire to test themselves against him. Even Todd Dillon kept in his place though Will had no doubt if he were given an opportunity to get even he wouldn't hesitate to jump at the chance. The Duffy boys had apologized to Will and Becky and had distanced themselves from Todd.

Ben and Running Bird took to Becky right away and accepted her as one of the gang. Wayne was a little hesitant because of what his brother had done and was relieved to find her accepting of him. The only activity she was not welcome at was swimming, due to the nature of their swimming attire, or lack of such. She took great pleasure in threatening to sneak up on them to steal their cloths but never carried it out.

Helen and Nathan loved her as a daughter. She worked hard and made life much more pleasant for Helen as she assumed much of the responsibility of running the boarding house. With Becky taking on so much of the work and the part time help of Mrs. Dillon, Helen and Nathan were free to pursue other interests. They didn't know it yet but their attention was being drawn to a subject that was on the mind of Will also, the plight of the Indians.

Chapter 7

A S THE DAYS of summer passed a new family was born. Each member found his place, and a closeness and security developed that permeated the Penny home. The Cully's chose to remain, at least for a while, at the boarding house and found a place for themselves also in the family circle.

One morning, towards fall, Will received a message that Bernie, down at the Ferry crossing, had something he wanted to show him. When he arrived Bernie took him to an old shed out back and pointed out what looked at first like a pile of rags. Looking closer Will could see that it was alive, then as his eyes began to pierce the gloom he gave a start. He was looking at the splitting image of Happy. Instinctively Will whistled and said "Come here Happy." To his amazement the dog jumped up and came straight for him. He knew the dog had to be an offspring of Happy. The only difference was that this dog had a truly happy disposition.

Will was in for another surprise. The dog turned and gave a little bark toward the corner from which he had just come, and in response out came the biggest cat Will had ever seen. He could only stare in disbelief as the two animals began to roughhouse together. One minute it was as if two dogs were tumbling over each other and the next minute they were stalking and pouncing on each other like cats would. "Isn't that about the most happy go lucky pair you have ever seen?" asked Bernie.

A few minutes later Will approached his home followed by a dog and cat named Happy and Lucky. As it would happen Helen and Nathan were sitting on the veranda with Becky, and Ben who had just arrived. Ben was the first to notice Will and his companions. He gave a visible start and let out a gasp when his eyes rested on Happy. Confusion took control of his brain momentarily as he first thought the dog was actually Happy, then he realized it was just an extraordinary look alike. He gave Will a questioning smile as his eyes misted over. "Where did you get that dog Will?"

Will explained that both the cat and dog had been hanging around Bernies' place for several days. Both Will and Bernie were positive the dog was an offspring of Happy. "He's yours if you want him Ben." Ben approached the dog who sat with his head down, as if sensing the emotions of Ben, then as Ben began to rub his neck he looked directly into his eyes. This was too much for Ben to deal with in front of his friends. Reaching down he picked the dog up and began walking toward the river. The dog though uncomfortable with his legs pinned beneath Ben's arms made no move or effort to free himself.

As they watched Ben disappear Will told Becky about how Wade Dillon had killed Happy. Will was surprised at the emotion Ben had displayed. It was over a year since he lost his dog and it was obvious that Ben had not yet gotten over it. Becky commented that Ben was obviously very tender hearted.

There were some major changes occurring in Will's world. Ben was preparing to go to New York to study medicine and would be gone for several years. While feeling a great sense of grief and loss Will was also supportive of Ben, and happy for the opportunity he had to go to one of the best schools in the nation. This was due to the efforts of Ruth Love and Richard Miller, who had campaigned tirelessly on his behalf to make this possible.

Added to Will's sense of loss was the departure of Running Bird. He had become more and more restless and dissatisfied in spite of Will's efforts to help him see the good things in his life. Running Bird saw only the unfairness and the mistreatment of a whole segment of society. He stole into Will's room late one night to say farewell. Will was not too surprised when he was awakened by Running Bird. He often came to Will's room when he had things on his mind. Running Bird, as usual chose to make his entrance through the window, and as usual landed on his stomach with a thud. Will smiled as he helped his friend dust himself off, then he waited for him to share what was on his mind.

This night he sat quietly for some time absently toying with a small silver bird attached to a leather strand he wore around his neck. As the moonlight glinted off of it he looked at Will. "This little bird is all I have left of my past. My father is dead; killed by drunk white men; my mother died giving me life; and all that my grandmother had for me is what you see in my hand." Running Bird's fingers turned blue as he nervously wound the cord around them, cutting off the circulation. "I want to find my place...someone who knows who I am, and where I belong."

"There is someone who knows you," answered Will, "and you don't have to leave to find Him."

Running Bird gazed at Will sharply, "I don't want to hear about your Jesus; You're my friend but I must find my own way, not yours!"

Running Bird left as the sun was beginning to lighten the sky. The worst of it for Will was the knowledge that his friend was not even sure where he was going. He only knew there was a place for him somewhere and he would find it. Will had not been able to make Running Bird see that what he was seeking would never be found in a place but in a relationship, a relationship with his Creator.

The loss of his friends drove Will closer to Becky. She was his confidant and best friend. He hid nothing from her. In turn she drew strength and security from him. It was only natural that they would begin to look toward the future together. They had discovered a little grassy knoll, well shaded, that overlooked the river. They spent many an hour there watching Happy and Lucky play, sharing their dreams and making plans for their future.

Lucky and Becky had become friends immediately and Ben had asked Will to keep Happy for him. Will and Becky enjoyed the two unique animals. The oneness and seeming singleness of purpose demonstrated by the two animals presented a pattern for Becky and Will. They actually agreed on everything except one topic. Will missed the desert. It had become a part of him and he had a conviction that his future and Becky's were somehow connected with the desert. Becky feared it. She saw it as a place of bareness and death and wanted no part of it for herself or for Will.

In consideration for Becky, Will kept his thoughts and plans, in respect to the desert, to himself. He would deal with it when the time came. In the meantime they both had plenty to keep them busy. Becky had another year of school to complete then she planned to go to teachers college in San Diego. Will was working hard, putting money aside, and laying plans for providing a livelihood for him and Becky. He was conscious of an ever- present conviction that he and Becky would somehow be involved with the Indians, providing help and a chance for them to better their condition.

⤜ ⤛

The year passed quickly, and with its passage came maturity to Will. He was a man with a purpose and a determination to see that purpose fulfilled. He was also haunted by the fact that Running Bird had disappeared into the desert and no one knew where he was. Will was determined he was going to find him. There was another matter that haunted Will, the mystery of Crazy Tom Pound. From time to time reports would drift in that he had been located. Usually he would suddenly appear at a lonely camp site and stay just long enough to purchase supplies; then he would disappear again.

Will could not free himself from the sense of tragedy and loss that overshadowed him when he thought about the man hopelessly wondering the desert seeking what had been lost so long ago. And what of the wife and son who had waited in vain for so many years? What thoughts and visions haunted their dreams? Will was determined he was going to find the answer.

Chapter 8

WILL THOUGHT HE was prepared for Becky's departure for Teachers College but he found out different the morning she was to leave. He awoke to find himself overwhelmed by a sense of foreboding and emptiness. He told himself it was but for a season and necessary to their future but there was no stilling the storm that was raging within him. He felt awkward and unsure of himself as he took her to the stage depot. Becky was quiet also, struggling with her own emotions. She knew she had to be strong but the strength she usually drew from Will seemed to have evaporated. She wondered how she could do without the strength and encouragement she received from him every day.

As they sat waiting for the stage they struggled for words. There was so much to be said yet no words could be found to say it. It was almost a relief when the stage rolled to a stop and the passengers luggage was stowed on top. It was a relief laced with panic as Will helped Becky into the passengers compartment. He wanted to yank her back out and run away with her but her hand was wrested from him and the door was slammed shut by the driver. It was as though his very life's blood was draining away as he helplessly watched the coach slowly begin to roll, then pick up speed. He stood waving, his face frozen in a corpse like smile as he fought to control the tears that threatened to burst their boundaries.

Will remained still for some time unwilling to face the rest of the day. Finally, as the dust settled and all trace of the coach, and Becky disappeared, he turned and slowly walked home. He knew if he was going to survive the coming year he must keep busy. But he must be busy with the right things. As he walked he began to lay out his plans. As soon as the weather cooled he would look for Running Bird. Even without the concern for his friend there was something compelling him to loose himself for a while in the desert wilderness where he had learned so much about himself and where the principles of life had been made so clear to him.

So he returned to his routine while preparing for his adventure. He faithfully answered every letter from Becky. He cherished her letters and sought to keep her informed of all the happenings at home but was careful not to mention his preparations or plans to go into the desert. He would deal with that in due time.

Will talked his plans over with Nathan. This trip was to be different and would pose dangers unlike his other trips into the desert. This time he would be alone, a fact that caused his mother much concern. The loss of a horse or an injury could prove fatal to a man on his own. Added to this was the fact that Will was going into territory totally new to him. He needed to learn the locations of the water holes as well as a general description of the land and any areas to avoid.

There was also the unresolved issue of hostile Indians. Having been driven off their land and pretty much subdued prior to 1860, they had taken advantage of the US Army's preoccupation with the South during the Civil war, reclaiming land and chasing settlers out. Even now several years later there were still small bands wandering in the desert, robbing and killing any white man they found on land they felt was rightfully theirs.

Nathan had another concern. Thad Dillon was out of jail and he and his two oldest sons, Wade and Todd, had been causing trouble. Nathan was convinced it was only a matter of time until they would turn their attention to Will. It would be a simple matter to follow him into the desert and kill him while no one would ever know what happened. Will had taken to wearing a gun and also practiced with it to keep himself sharp.

Nathan had given Will one of his horses, named Chalky. He was a good one, strong and rugged, well suited for desert travel, having been raised and trained by a Choctaw Indian. He loved horses and knew how to break them without breaking their spirit. All that was left for Will was to gain his confidence. It was not long before the two were totally devoted to one another. Will also purchased a good mule to carry all he would need to survive in the desert. The only potential problem was water since it was impossible to carry enough for himself and the animals.

When all preparations were complete Will sat down to one last task. He must let Becky know what he was doing. His words came slow at first, and dealt only with routine things a young man writes to his girl. Then he got to the main point:

> By the time you get this letter I will be in the desert. I realize this may hurt you and will certainly cause you worry but it is something I must do. I owe it to Running Bird and I know now that I could never live with myself if somethingbad happened to him and I had not tried. Rest assured I have prepared well and know the risks and will take no foolish chances. I will feel safer if I know you are saying a prayer for me from time to time.

Will finished the letter and sealed it up. He felt a sense of guilt knowing that he had taken the easy way out by waiting until she was gone and then writing a letter, but he had not had the heart to broach the subject when he knew she would never consent willingly to such a trip. As he posted the letter he breathed a prayer to accompany it, hoping she would find comfort in his assurances of caution.

Will left home the next morning heading north east. He felt that Running Bird may be in one of the several mountain ranges located in that area. He followed the Gila River for the first couple of days then he turned just about due north, a move that soon put him in unfamiliar country. It didn't take long before Will began to feel alone and vulnerable. It seemed like every shrub or rock hid an enemy just waiting for the opportunity to jump out at him. Every noise and movement was amplified and he felt an oppressiveness he had never before experienced anywhere.

Will finally had enough. Taking an army telescope given him by Nathan, he went to the top of a little knoll and began a sweeping survey of the surrounding area. He looked in vain for any indication of movement; the glint of the sun reflecting off of steel or some tell tale dust or smoke, but he saw nothing. He did see a small rock formation some sixty feet high and about a quarter of a mile long. He immediately recognized it as one of the places where he would find water. He guessed it to be some two hours walking distance and decided to make that his camp for the night.

The fact that he had a goal in sight and the knowledge he was on course melted Will's apprehension and returned the sense of optimism that he had been feeling earlier. He returned to his animals and gave each one a good drink then he began making his way toward his destination encouraged by the anticipation of a good rest.

As the afternoon wore on it became obvious to Will that he had missed on his estimate of two hours distance to his camp site. Along with a mild sense of disappointment came a renewed sense of uneasiness. This time it was different. Something was not right. He noticed that the animals were also restless. For the first time in over an hour he turned his attention toward the west and he knew immediately that he was in trouble. The whole horizon was obscured in a yellowish brown haze of rolling, boiling activity. Will immediately got on his horse and urged him into a lope. He knew better than to run his animals but he also knew the consequences of being caught without shelter in a dust storm.

The animals, motivated by an instinctive sense of fear, quickened their pace, forcing Will to restrain them. As he fought his horse and mule, holding them back, he kept his eyes on his destination. The small but all-important place of shelter drew near ever so slowly; too slowly for Will so he gave Chalky a little more slack. He could sense the panic beginning to rise under his saddle as their pace quickened.

Will was determined not to give in to the urge to run full out. He also determined he would not look behind him. He would hold to an even pace they could maintain and keep his eyes on his goal. He was doing quite well until he heard Blacky snort and then bolt. The mule's sudden jerk on the rope almost upset him and Chalky. The air was getting heavy and dark and the odor of dust began to fill his nostrils. He could not resist any longer and turned to look at the monster bearing down on him.

It was only a matter of minutes until they would be overtaken, and Will knew he must work fast. He quickly gave the animals another drink then he cut a short length of rope and tied one end to the pommel of his saddle and the other end around his wrist. His fate was now tied to that of his horse and he knew he must trust him completely. He hastily wrapped a bandana around his face and once again headed for the rocks, only now he trotted between the two animals knowing they would break the wind a little bit and provide some shelter.

When the storm overtook them it was with a fury that Will never would have imagined. He found himself in the midst of a blinding, smothering rage of wind and dust. He began gasping and choking, struggling for air, unable to see. He fought to maintain control of his senses but his world was spinning and he soon lost all track of time or sense of direction. The roar of the storm threatened to burst his ear drums and the sand laden wind tore at his clothing and face. It was as though he was being dragged and bumped and carried along into a huge black swirling, vortex of pain, helplessness, and terror. He was running a gauntlet of howling demons, spitting fire and brimstone at him, causing his face and eyes to burn, sucking every bit of breath out of his lungs, and all the while seeking to knock his feet out from under him.

Suddenly it felt like his arm was being torn out of its socket as his feet vainly sought solid footing. Will buried his face into the heaving hairy mass to which he was melded and succumbed to his fate. He knew he was suffocating. His last thoughts were of Becky and his mind shouted out begging for her forgiveness. He shouted a prayer heard only by God, "Please look after Becky!" then came oblivion.

When consciousness returned to Will he found himself wedged tightly between Chalky and the mule. He first became aware of the pain in his arm and shoulder then he realized he was sharing a small crevice with his animals. Somehow Chalky had led them through the storm and found this place of safety.

It was some time before Will could work his way from between the animals. He wondered how they were able to wedge themselves into such a tight place. As he backed Chalky out the first thing he noticed was the sand caked in his eyes and nostrils. Taking a canteen he carefully cleaned them out, then he did the same for Blacky. When he had given them both a drink he turned his attention on himself. His face was sore and he felt like he had been in a stampede. Any use of his right arm brought immediate pain.

He realized he had been dragged for some distance then had hung between the two animals all night. He also realized they had saved his life. It was full daylight and there was no trace of the storm that had overtaken them the evening before.   Will took stock of their situation. He must find water soon as he had emptied the last canteen. He was pretty sure they were close to the spring he had been headed for yesterday. He just had to decide whether to head east or west. He decided to trust the decision to Chalky's sense of smell but after a few steps the horse seemed confused. With a chill, Will realized there was no water close enough to provide a scent for the horse to follow.

The best thing to do was to find a vantage point from which he could search for signs of water and they might as well head east. They walked along the base of the rock wall for about an hour and had covered a couple of miles, when off to the left they saw what they were looking for. Tucked into a break in the rock face was a little oasis with green grass, shade trees and a clear flowing spring. It didn't occur to Will that this was a much larger up-thrust than the formation he had been focused on the day before. He thought only of the water. The weary, dusty travelers wasted no time in quenching their thirst, and Will was soon stretched out under a shady bush, sound asleep, while his companions were satisfying their hunger on the lush green grass.

Will remained at the spring that day and the next, resting and scouting around. It hadn't taken too long to figure out that he had missed his target during the storm. Consequently he had no idea were he was. On the afternoon of the second day he climbed onto a rock outcropping seeking some familiar landmark that would give him his bearing. As he sat scanning the desert floor he gradually became aware of several buzzards some distance away. Taking his glass he pinpointed something but it was too far away to tell what it was. He assumed it was an animal of some kind but decided he should check it out to be sure.

It was some time before Will had saddled Chalky and ridden out to where the carcass lay. As he came near his skin suddenly began to crawl. Before him lay a small donkey and a few feet beyond it the body of a man. He was old and his outfit showed evidence of many miles of travel and many years of use in the desert. Will sat quietly as a pall of sadness engulfed him. He knew who it was. It could only be Crazy Tom Pound.

The scene before him gave testimony that he had been trapped by the same storm that had almost taken Will's life. His face was still wrapped in a bandanna. Closer examination revealed that his eyes and ears, as well as his mouth, were filled with sand. The flimsy neck scarf was no match for the wind driven sand. He had tried to dig a shelter but it was in vain as the wind filled it in as quickly as the desperate man could shovel it out. He lay with teeth clenched and hands wrapped around the shovel handle.

Will finally dismounted and approached the dead man. He would bury him, but first he must go through his things to see if there was any way to identify his wife. There may also be something that would be valued by her. The rest he would bury with the body. He found a few coins and about seventy five dollars worth of gold, a broken watch, and two letters. One was from his wife, post marked some ten years earlier, and one was from Tom addressed to his wife but never sent. It too appeared to be several years old and was still sealed.

The letter to Tom had been opened. Will struggled with his conscience. He had no desire to intrude into the private matters of others, but he felt he needed some guidance, and therefore was justified looking into the open envelope. The first item was a newspaper clipping announcing that Corporal Thomas Pound was missing in action at the battle of Antietam and presumed dead. Along with the clipping was a letter from the US War department, addressed to Mrs. Mary Pound, giving official verification and some details of the incident that suggested he was dead.

Will assumed Mary must be the mother of Thomas and wife of the dead prospector but upon reading the other letter in the envelope he discovered that Mary was actually the wife of Thomas Pound. The tragedy of Crazy Tom Pound was made all too clear as Will read the letter from his wife. One paragraph stood out and seemed to sum up the sad story.

I have no way of knowing if you are alive or dead. I send this letter General Delivery not really believing it will find you, but in so doing I fulfill my last obligation to you. You should know of the death of our son, and that he left a lovely wife, Mary and two sons, Phillip and Andrew. I have waited and hoped for your return for too many years. Now I am beginning a new chapter in my life. I am an old woman, but have been offered a chance for love by a dear Gentleman who loves me and will provide the care and security I so desperately need. I will marry him one week from today. If by chance this letter finds you don't bother answering it as I finally consider you dead.

Will sat in silent shock as the impact of the letter and the tragic story it told became clear. Here was a man who had everything anyone could desire yet he had thrown it all away for the sake of a season of self-gratification. One little misguided choice had led to heart-break, and loneliness and the loss of the love and closeness that his wife and son, and later two grandsons held out to him.

Will buried every item belonging to Tom Pound with his body, except the letter he had written and never sent. He was determined that nothing would remain to interfere with the women's happiness and peace of mind. He also vowed never to speak of him or reveal that he had found him. It was better that the mystery of Crazy Tom Pound remain just that, a mystery. He wasn't sure why he kept the letter but for some reason he was compelled to keep it.

Back at camp Will turned his attention to his own problem, that of finding out where he was. He sat pondering the hand drawn map Nathan had made for him trying to discern which mountain range on the map corresponded with the one he could see off in the distance. After some indecision he plotted his course and settled down to rest. They would resume their journey in the morning, continuing their north east direction until they reached the Kofa mountain range. Then Will hoped to meet some friendly Indians and perhaps learn something of Running Bird's whereabouts.

Chapter 9

WILL TOOK HIS time with the chores and breakfast. He was in no hurry to leave the safety of the little oasis. He knew he must though and after a last check of the hooves and shoes of the animals he finally got under way. He was reasonably sure of where he was headed and told himself he would find water by nightfall. The animals were well rested, as was Will, and he was soon possessed by an optimistic spirit. As the day wore on Will kept his eyes open for landmarks resembling those sketched on his map, as well as any sign of man, whether it be tracks or dust or any other indication that he was nearing human habitation.

He went to sleep that night disappointed and a little concerned that he had to settle for a dry camp. He was forced to acknowledge that he had traveled farther than he thought during the sandstorm and consequently was lost. He estimated that he would reach the next range of mountains by noon the next day and surely find water. As he lay on his bedroll he struggled to subdue the exasperation that he felt. He was tempted to saddle up and continue on but he knew he might have a long day tomorrow. He had to find water or they would be in trouble. He also considered retracing his steps and returning to the oasis but that would be admitting defeat, besides he still didn't know where to go from there.

The next day was similar to the one before. Nothing was going as it should. They were almost out of water and both man and animals were thirsty, tired, and irritable. Will found himself arguing with Chalky and complaining to Blacky. When he discovered what he was doing he was forced to smile at himself, and his one sided conversation. He reached down to rub the horses neck as a gesture of apology and was surprised to be greeted by a violent jerk of his head as if he wasn't ready to patch things up yet.

They continued on for some time until they reached the crest of a rise, which gave, Will a good view for several miles. What he saw was hardly encouraging. The map was useless because Will could see nothing before him that resembled anything Nathan had drawn. Will felt a sudden clutch at his throat as the realization hit him that he was indeed lost, and in deep trouble.

As he sat staring he prayed. It was a simple prayer. "Father I need your help, please show me the way." Then he began retracing his steps in his mind, beginning when he left the Gila River. Trouble started when the dust storm had overtaken them. If only they had made it to the right water hole, or had not gone so far off course during the storm. Maybe they were lost because they had found the oasis so easily and were fooled into thinking they were on the right track. There had to be a reason. At this point Will began to be angry. He needed a reason why this was happening to him.

He had done all the right things and yet they had turned out bad. Before he knew it he was blaming God. Then he remembered something   his mom had said one time, "There is a good reason for everything that happens and if you trust God He will bring something good out of every situation." Will wondered how any good could come out of him being lost, with no water in the middle of the desert, and invited God to give him some answers.

The answer came loud and clear; so clear and sudden that it startled Will. Had he actually heard a voice? "Must you know the reason before you will trust me?" Though he didn't know where it came from he knew who it came from. It wasn't the kind of response he had expected but he now knew what the real issue was.

With that the battle was joined. Would he submit to anything, even being lost? Would he trust God to use every situation to accomplish His purposes? Would he be willing even to die, if God so chose? Will knew he was being asked to decide if he would submit completely to God, trusting Him for his life and future. Who was going to be Lord, God or himself? He knew it was his right to choose but much rested on his decision.

It took a long time for the battle to be decided. In the end Will simply said yes to God. He didn't know how long he had been staring into the desert. Nor did he know how long he had been aware of the slight movement that now arrested his full attention. It was too far off to be certain but it looked like a horse and rider. Will went into action immediately, realizing he must not squander this opportunity. By heading northwest he could intercept the rider within an hour. As he mounted Chalky, Will caught a glimpse of more movement farther to the South East. It looked like the dust of several horses and could mean only one thing. The lone rider was being chased. This cast a whole new light on the situation, telling Will he must exercise caution.

He wasted no time but he was careful not to be seen by the approaching riders, keeping to the low ground and taking advantage of the cover provided by trees and what little brush there was. He wanted to find out who the lone rider was. Better to deal with one person than six or seven. It took longer than he thought it would to overtake the fleeing rider and situate himself in a safe spot where he knew he could head him off. He found a place where the brush and rocks created a natural chute through which a horse and rider must come slowly and carefully, then he waited. It was only a short time before he heard the hoof beats and then the heavy breathing of the winded horse. With perfect timing Will stepped out and caught the horses bridal, then looked up into the startled eyes of a young Indian girl.

"Don't be afraid, I'm here to help you," said Will. He was not sure how far the pursuers were behind the girl so he didn't waste time with introductions. He assumed she was an innocent fugitive and if he learned different he would handle it later. He quickly instructed the girl to continue riding up a draw that she was just about to enter when Will had stopped her. Will would go around it and meet her farther up. That way the pursuers would not see any extra tracks and be alerted of his presence.

Will hurried toward a ridge of rocks that looked suitable for what he had planned and reached it at the same time the girl arrived. He quickly explained what they were going to do then set about his task. The riders would follow the girl's tracks up the draw to where the trail again narrowed down forcing them to ride single file, making a perfect location for an ambush. He knew it was risky but he made three small fires seeking to create a bed of red hot coals in each, then he gave the girl one of his revolvers and instructed her to open fire at the riders when she heard him shooting. He placed her where she could not be seen but where she had an unobstructed view. Will hoped the riders would think they were being attacked by a large force and turn and run.

Working quickly Will grabbed his Winchester and some extra boxes of shells and found a safe vantage point where he could see the approaching riders in plenty of time. He didn't have long to wait. They came slowly and deliberately eyes fixed on the tracks of the girl's pony. At the first sign of them Will went to each fire and dropped a handful of shells into the coals. He then hurried back to his rifle praying that the timing would be right. If it was the men would be in for a surprise.

Even at their deliberate pace it seemed that they covered the ground quickly, almost too quickly for Will's comfort. He broke out into a sweat as he got a good look at the face of Thad Dillon, and got set for the worst. There was a point at which he must open fire whether the shells did their part or not and Thad was nearing that point. Will tried to estimate how long the cartridges had been in the coals but he had lost track of time. He took careful aim. He hated to do it but he knew he must kill at least two of the horses, and preferably three. The crack of Will's rifle was followed by gun fire from the direction of the girl, and to Will's surprise two horses immediately fell dead spilling their riders. Then the cartridges began to explode. Another shot by Will and another horse fell.

The bandits were filled with panic and as a group turned and ran for their lives, thinking they had been attacked by several men. For a while all was confusion and chaos as the men on foot shouted and swore at their mounted cohorts to come back and pick them up. It wasn't until they felt they were out of range that they finally stopped and waited for them to catch up. Then they rode away as fast as the overloaded horses could take them.

Will sat quietly for some time. There had been six men in all, Thad, Todd, and Wade Dillon, and three of the kidnapers of Myron Hamilton. When he was sure they were not going to return he went to search for the girl and was not surprised to find her laying on the ground beside her horse sound asleep. It was then he noticed her condition. She was obviously exhausted, her clothes were torn and she was bruised and scraped. The black circles around her eyes gave testimony of her lack of sleep. It took some time for her to wake up. Then she remembered where she was. Will immediately saw the fear in her eyes and her agitation increased by the minute. She had obviously been mistreated.

He assured her that he was a friend and began to ask her questions about herself. His relaxed manner soon had its effect on her and she calmed down. Will suggested that they would be wise to be on their way.

Looking at Will the girl said, "We must get to water. It's just a short way from here." Will felt a mixture of relief and consternation. He was relieved that they had water but troubled that he had not been able to locate it. It wasn't long before they were safe in a hidden gully with all the water and grass they would need.

Will was anxious to learn who the young girl was and why she was being chased by Dillon and his gang of cutthroats but he waited until she was ready to talk about it. It wasn't until they had finished supper that she began to talk. Her name was Terisa, a Yuma Indian. She had learned English by working at a trading post and mission school. It had closed down when the couple running it had grown too old to continue and had moved to Phoenix.

Terisa was returning to her village when she stumbled into the camp of Thad Dillon and had immediately become his prisoner. "I don't know what would have happened if it hadn't been for the youngest member of the gang. It was almost as if he was a prisoner himself. It was he who saved me." Will looked startled at Terisa,

"Do you know his name?" "Yes, it was Wayne." "Do you know where he is now?" asked Will his voice heavy with fear.

With that the girl's eyes fell. "They were all drinking and getting uglier by the minute. They began mocking him. The leader said he was going to make a man of him. When it got dark Wayne crept out of the camp and turned all but two horses loose. When he thought the others were drunk enough, he cut me loose and we made a run for it."

"What happened to Wayne?" Terisa sat, unable to speak, her mouth seeking to form words that would not come. Finally she said, "as we rode away they began shooting...I Think he's dead."

"You think he's dead?" Hope began to replace the dread in Will's heart.

Once again the girl struggled to speak. "They shot him in the back. I saw the blood fly out of his chest when the bullet came through."

Will stumbled out of camp and began running. When he was out of earshot of Terisa he fell on his face and gave vent to the grief and anger that tore at his soul. He cried until he had no more strength or tears left, then his thoughts turned to Thad Dillon.

Anger, hate, and vengeance roared through his being like a blast furnace threatening to take control of him and destroy the caring and compassion that usually characterized him. As he became aware of the feelings dominating him he became frightened for they revealed a capacity, and a side of his nature he had been, up until now, unaware of. It filled him with dread and he knew he must cleanse his soul. Finally, totally spent he lay still and quietly began to talk to his Creator. He didn't ask "why", Rather he asked "what!" What should he do? He asked for guidance and strength to save the girl and himself, for he knew without a doubt Thad Dillon would be after them.

The next thing he was aware of was a hand on his shoulder shaking him awake. It was broad daylight. "We must go. I have food ready and everything is packed." With that Terisa turned and walked back to camp. They rode hard all day, the girl leading the way. They were headed for the safety of her village. She knew the way, and she knew where the water was. Will was thankful for the opportunity to follow. He was able to ponder and think about what had taken place. He did have the presence to check their back trail regularly to guarantee they were not overtaken.

As they rode Will thought about Wayne. How could a man take the life of his own son? Will was once again filled with revulsion as he considered Thad Dillon. He was well aware of the hate and cruelty that drove him but he wasn't aware of the feelings that the man was experiencing at this moment.

Not too many miles from where Will and the girl made camp that night was another campfire. Five men sat around it. The sixth man lay dead with a bullet from Thad Dillon's gun in his head. When Wayne and Terisa made their escape Thad began shooting over their heads and instructed the others to do so also, hoping that it would frighten the pair into stopping. Murphy had always hated Wayne and seeing his opportunity, he shot him. Everyone assumed it had been an accident until Murphy drank too much. Liquor always made him talk too much and this time was no exception, and retribution came quick.

Thad Dillon was a contradiction to all that was good in humanity. He was guided by selfishness and motivated by a sinister and dark passion that would manifest itself in violent outbursts without warning. His sense of right and wrong was not based upon any moral code but upon his feelings and opinions. His grief for his son was genuine but it was accompanied by a perverted sense of right and wrong. His sorrow over the murder of Wayne justified the shooting of Murphy. Any remorse or regret for his actions was replaced by revenge, which, in his view condoned his behavior.

He felt no responsibility for the mistreatment of Terisa, because to him she was nothing more the a second class person put upon this earth for the pleasure of people like him.

Thad Dillon also had an intense hatred for Will Carter, whom he considered ultimately responsible for the death of Wayne. It was Will who had lured his son away and planted strange ideas in his head, turning him against his own father. Thad Dillon was determined to kill Will Carter and he wanted to waste no time in getting it done.

Terisa had been exhausted by her ordeal but she was strong and recovered well even as they traveled. Will found her to be intelligent and confident. As they lay in their bedrolls they talked about the events of the past couple of days and how he had arrived just in time to rescue her.

"How did you know where I was going and what to do?" she asked. Will explained that he was watching from a high vantage point. He could see where she had been, where she was in relation to her enemies, and where she was headed. "I could see from horizon to horizon," he said "and knew just what had to be done."

"It must be wonderful to be such a friend with God. He was the only one with a better view than you." she answered "Your view was limited only by time, the Creator sits so high that He can see past the horizons of time. He knows the beginning from the end."

Will lay speechless. His mind reeled at the profound wisdom the girl had just spoken. He went back to his confrontation with God and it all began to weave together into a pattern.

Terisa was in trouble. God, in his wisdom had placed Wayne in the right place at the right time to protect her and gain her freedom. She would need help the next day so God placed Will in the right place at the right time through a series of "random" happenings that had made no sense to him. In the end everything had fit together properly, because of the hand putting each piece of the puzzle in place.

Will had a couple more question. What about Tom Pound, and Wayne? Why did they have to die? Once again Will was reminded that God saw things in light of eternity. Death is a natural part of the working out of the master plan. While it brings separation and grief, it is never the less only temporary for God's children. When a person begins to view his life in terms of eternity and God's sovereign love, he can live in the confidence that all things will be made to work for ultimate good. Even the bad and unfair things are turned to the ultimate good in time. Will took comfort in the knowledge that he would see Wayne again.

Will was disappointed that Terisa had not heard of Running Bird. She felt certain, though, that if he was anywhere near her brother Walking Horse would know of him. Will found the name Walking Horse quite unusual so Terisa explained that even the swiftest of horses is of no value unless it is sure-footed and careful on the high places and dangerous trails. Her brother was strong and capable to act when action was needed but he was also thoughtful and careful. For that reason he was able to avoid trouble and provide leadership to those who depended upon him.

Walking Horse used the name Stone Walker, when he was away from the village doing business in the white mans world.

Will saw the obvious respect the girl had for her brother and commented that he sounded like a chief. "Yes, he would have made a great chief" Terisa responded wistfully.

Will would have explored the topic further but Terisa changed the subject. "Tomorrow", she said "we will travel hard and the next day we will be home." With that she turned over and went to sleep.

Will eased out of camp and went to the horses. He stood for some time talking to Chalky who nodded his head as though he understood every word. Will was uneasy. What had become of Thad Dillon and his gang? He decided to keep watch for at least part of the night just in case. He found a good viewpoint and made himself comfortable and let his mind wonder as he gazed out over the sleeping desert.

It was not long before Will began to think about Becky. He had grown accustomed to the dull ache that had taken residency in his heart. He missed her terribly and wondered how she was getting along. As his eyes grew heavy he caught visions of her smiling face and the musical laugh that always warmed his heart. It was almost as if he was walking hand in hand with her again and a warmth began to wash over him.

Suddenly his eyes flew open as a wave of fear engulfed him. Something had brought him awake. Afraid to breathe, he sat perfectly still. Then he heard it again, the scuff of a boot against stone. Someone was out in the darkness, seeking to creep up on their camp. Will scolded himself for leaving his gun in camp. He had to get back before the person, whoever it was, could get there.

After crawling for a good distance Will figured it would be safe to stand up. He ran quietly until he reached the camp and retrieved his revolver. Then he nudged Terisa with his foot and motioned for her to keep quiet and concealed himself. He would give the intruder a reception he would not forget. Suddenly Will went cold as it dawned on him that the first place the person would go to would be the horses. He was just about to head for them when he heard a shot and a startled and angry cry of pain. Then there was a sound of someone crashing through the bushes and in a few moments the beating hooves of a horse galloping away.

Will was furious with himself and also humiliated that he had been so foolish not to immediately think about the horses. He realized he had much to learn. He was also thankful to see Terisa leading the animals into camp. It was easy to figure out that Dillon had sent at least one of his men to get the horses. If he had succeeded it would be relatively easy to do away with Will and Terisa. After a short discussion they agreed that they should head out right away. They knew that the Dillons were still short of mounts so they could not keep up with them; but they also knew they would probably be followed by one rider who would leave a trail for the rest to follow once they got horses.

They traveled hard all day and after a short rest that night they left early the next morning. Terisa had a good knowledge of tracking and she and Will used every opportunity and trick available to hide their trail. They were sure they had succeeded as several checks of their back-trail by Will had failed to reveal any sign of a rider. Will's confidence wavered though as he considered the fact that he had been checking their back-trail earlier and had not spotted the man following them. He was determined to be extra careful.

The day was long and Terisa was lost in her thoughts. Will was also bothered by something Terisa had said. She had referred to him as a friend of God. This was a rebuke to him. He began to think back upon his journey with his Creator.

Will remembered his early concept of God. He was his Heavenly Father; the one who took care of him and met his needs. Later he saw Him as the Ruler of all Creation; the one who set the rules and gave direction. It was not hard to bow to His Lordship. After all it didn't interfere with the every day issues of life. He could handle them himself and let God take care of the big things.

In his early teens Will began to see God as someone he could approach and know personally. He could talk to Him and listen to Him. This complicated his life a little bit. This meant he must be honest and keep nothing from God. He would be accountable for his attitude and his actions.

The concept of friendship with Jesus was a blow to his spiritual ego and part of him wanted to avoid it altogether. Will couldn't get Jesus' last night with His disciples out of his mind. He had asked them to remain with Him in His hour of need. Instead he was betrayed, denied, and deserted by those He counted dearest.

Will was almost overwhelmed with a strange foreboding that God was going to ask something terrible of him. Would he be faithful? Or would he desert His Savior like Peter did. One thing he knew, God would never ask anything of him He himself would not do for Will. He also knew God would never ask him to do anything or go anywhere alone. He would always be with him.

About mid afternoon they turned south and entered a little valley between two mountain ranges. As they followed the valley floor it climbed steadily until it became apparent to Will that they were approaching the summit of a pass. Each side of the pass was dominated by a high peak which sat as if quarding the valley below. Terisa identified them as Twin Eagle Peaks. To her, they were the gateway to home, and Will sensed the anticipation that was within her. She quickened the pace of her horse as they drew near the summit and finally let him run the last two hundred yards. Will smiled at her as he walked the last several feet to where she had stopped. He was struck by the expression on her face. Obviously she was looking at something that brought her joy. When he reached her side he looked to see what was having such a transforming effect on her.

He stood transfixed as he gazed at the sight before him. The trail fell away and the two mountain ranges continued on to the West forming another valley which Will guessed to be about five miles wide and about eight miles long. A mesa running East and West bound the Southern end of the valley between the two ranges of mountain. It's height and angle was such that it formed a barrier that no man could breech. As far as Will could see the only way into the valley was the way he and Terisa had come.

Will had seen valleys before, many of which were bigger and more inaccessible than this one. What made this one different were the colors. The mesquite, greasewood, and creosote bush of the desert had given way to lush green grass, trees, and other vegetation that Will could not identify.

"Now I know what Eden was like" he murmured. "I can hardly believe what I am seeing...What place is this?"

"The elders call it the Valley of Refuge, the younger ones call it The Land of Promise. We know it is our last stronghold against the white man who is seeking to take all our land from us."

Terisa bent down and took a hand full of dirt, then holding it out in front of her she let it pour from her hand. She then took another handful and stood facing Will. Once again she poured the dirt out. She explained that it was a signal to those guarding the approach to the village that she was one of them and was bringing nothing or no one that would threaten the safety of the people. She had also identified Will as a friend who was no threat.

Before Will could blink, it seemed, six mounted braves encircled them. The looks he received caused Will to break out into a sweat as he realized that Terisa stood between him and death. She immediately explained what had happened to her and that Will had saved her from the Dillon gang. Without a word they led Terisa and Will down the slope and into the village.

As they rode they passed fields of corn, melons of all kinds, and other vegetables as well as grapes and citrus trees. Will was sorely tempted to take an orange or melon and savor it's sweet juice but he feared he may be breaking some sort of protocol so he stayed stiff lipped on his horse until they reached the center of the village.

Terisa was at once surrounded by laughing, smiling faces as friends and relatives welcomed her home and started peppering her with questions. A sudden hush fell over the crowed as they began to understand what had happened to her and they began looking at Will in a new light. He was a friend and benefactor and must be treated as such. He was shown to a small but adequate adobe hut and told that was where he would sleep. He was also informed that he would eat the evening meal with Terisa's family, including Silver Hair, the chief of the village.

It didn't take long for Will to figure out that he would not be leaving the village all that soon. He was one of very few white men who had seen it and the Indians were determined to keep it's location, and hopefully its existence, secret.

The following day Will was given a tour by Silver Hair and Walking Horse. Silver Hair explained that three generations of his family had lived here. The valley was watered by a huge spring that gushed up through a subterranean passage in the base of one of the twin peaks. The valley supported one hundred and fifty people quite easily. Besides a variety of produce they raised sheep and some cattle. As they continued on Will sensed that he was under scrutiny. Both of his hosts paid close attention to any response Will made and from time to time asked questions. Before he knew it he realized he had told them about Nathan and his mother as well as Becky.

Will stayed in the valley for a week. During that time he became friends with Silver Hair and Walking Horse. He also learned of the concern the chief and his grandson shared for the safety of their valley. They felt that it was only a matter of time before their right to ownership was challenged. Silver Hair admitted that he didn't have anything to prove ownership. Walking Horse had been to school and was a licensed lawyer. As such he had searched for a deed or old land grant, or anything that could establish a legitimate claim to title but it had been in vain.

Walking Horse vowed to continue the search and Will committed himself to help in any way he could. He also promised to keep the existence of the valley secret.

Chapter 10

WHEN IT WAS time for Will to leave the valley Terisa accompanied him part of the way, showing him a trail that took him to the South side of the mesa. As he looked around he was surprised to find himself in familiar territory and to his astonishment he realized he was less than forty miles from home. He was glad when he had covered those forty miles and arrived at home.

Will was disappointed that he had not found any trace of Running Bird. Walking Horse had promised to begin asking around and having friends do the same. He felt that eventually someone would turn up who knew him. When Will told Helen and Nathan about Wayne, Nathan insisted that they go immediately to Sheriff Moore. Will found it a little awkward not being able to reveal the whereabouts of Terisa, who was the only eyewitness other than the Dillon gang. He wasn't even able to tell him where the body could be found. In the end the Sheriff was forced to let the matter drop. Without a body there could be no charges laid.

Will knew the Dillon's would be looking for him now and he must be very careful. He felt frustrated and lonely. His days were long and aimless. Finally Helen suggested that he go to San Diego and visit Becky. Will thought it was a wonderful idea, one which he had already come up with. He let his mother take pleasure in the illusion that she had come to her sons rescue.

The journey to San Diego took two days of hard driving. The stage was dusty and bumpy, and was carrying two passengers too many. When he arrived he was tired and dusty, and hungry. He had a small travel bag and a slip of paper with the address of the home where Becky was staying.

After wandering around for some time and asking several people for directions he finally found the house. He almost fell as he rushed up the steps of the front porch. In his eagerness he failed to see Becky sitting on the porch swing until he was right before her. He heard a startled gasp, then "Will? Is that you Will?"

He turned with a smile but a cold chill wiped it off of his face, then he turned bright red. Becky was not alone. Sitting beside her was a young man, a little older than Will. Will was in a state of utter confusion, unable to utter a word. Becky stood to her feet as did the young man, both of them sensing the terrible awkwardness of the moment. Becky was overcome by a flood of compassion for Will and knew she must do or say something before the situation got out of hand.

Stepping forward she said "Will, I'm so surprised to see you." Will opened his mouth to respond but Becky wisely continued "Meet my friend Ory Middleton." Fate came to the rescue as the front door opened and a young women stepped through, "And this is his wife Marie." In his joy and relief Will lost all semblance of reserve or poise. With a huge smile he grabbed Ory's hand and shook it vigorously then he did the same to Marie. Then he grabbed Becky's hand and shook it too. Suddenly he was overcome with embarrassment as he realized what he had just done. He stood with a silly grin on his face unable to say a word. the other three stood dumbfounded for a moment, then they howled with laughter.

That broke the tension for Will and he joined them, not minding at all that they were laughing at him. After they were able to settle down Ory and Marie dismissed themselves. Will immediately grabbed Becky in his arms and picking her off her feet began twirling her around. Her laughter rang like music in his ears. They sat on the swing and Will explained the suddenness of his decision to come for a visit. He knew he must tell her about his desert experience also but was relieved when Mrs. Moffit announced that it was suppertime. She also graciously provided a room for Will while he was visiting. Will thanked her but insisted he would pay for his room as well as his meals. He knew what it was like to run a boarding house and try to make a living.

That evening Will told Becky all that had happened in the desert, leaving nothing out except the finding of Tom Pound. She wept when she learned of Wayne's death. Will comforted her as they talked late into the night. Becky found the whole desert trip upsetting but she had confidence in Will and knew she must not hold him too tight. She must let him make his decisions and trust his judgment. Will wanted to know all about her studies and the friends she had made. Of course much of what he heard had already been shared by letter but it sounded so much better in person.

The days flew by and it was suddenly time for Will to leave. The morning of his departure he walked Becky to school then made his way toward the stage depot, already dreading the long tiring trip that lay ahead. He wasn't paying attention to the people milling around him therefore he didn't hear when his name was called. The second time it came louder and with a tone that gave Will a sickening start. Looking up he gazed into the twisted face of Wade Dillon. Will was not prepared for a confrontation, a fact Wade sensed and which made him all the more determined to force Will into a fight. He intended to shoot him dead.

Will's first thought was of Wayne and he threw it into Wade's teeth. "Are you going to shoot me in the back like you did your brother?"

"What do you know about that?" retorted Wade. "The man who shot Wayne has a bullet in his head." By now people were taking notice of the confrontation and a small crowd had formed, fully expecting to see a fight.

Wade had no desire to discuss the things that had taken place in the desert in front of the curious crowd. On the other hand Will had no desire to participate in a gun fight, even if it was with Wade. Seeing his advantage he pressed it. "And what about the girl you mistreated?" Wade was becoming more uncomfortable as he sensed the crowd's agitation. Someone in the crowd suggested that the Sheriff should be informed and that Wade and Will be held until he arrived. In response Wade drew and fired into the dirt causing the

spectators to fall back and giving him a chance to break through the
circle and escape down an ally to where his horse was tied.

As Will sat waiting for the stage, the Sheriff who had heard about
the confrontation approached him. He wanted to know Wade's name
and what had happened to Wayne and Teresa. Will told him all he
knew leaving out only the existence and location of the Valley of
Refuge. Having learned all he could from Will and being satisfied
that there was really nothing he could do he cautioned Will to be
careful and left.

Will didn't rest at all on the journey home. He knew it would be
all too easy for Wade and a couple of his friends to stop the stage
coach and while holding it up kill him in the process. The journey
was uneventful except when four riders hailed it as it passed them
in the middle of the night.

The driver had no intention of stopping and the riders made no
effort to run the coach down. If it were Wade and friends they realized Will would be alerted and ready to defend himself by the time
they could stop the stage. On the other hand if it had stopped when
hailed Will may have been asleep and easy to deal with. Will was
relieved to get home without trouble. He assumed his enemies had
departed for safer territory but had no illusions that he was free of
their threats. He determined to get on with his life but with one eye
on his back trail at all times.

≫ ≪

It was getting close to spring and Will was looking forward to
seeing Ben who planned to come home for the summer break. He
was also anxious to see Becky who also planned to return in a short
time. In a way he was disappointed with himself. He had failed to
find Running Bird and he had not saved money or made solid plans
regarding his and Becky's future. He went back to work at the blacksmith shop and while keeping his hands busy he also occupied his
mind planning and wondering what the future had for them.

For some reason the valley of refuge was constantly on Will's
mind. He began to wonder if his future may be somehow connected
with the valley and it's inhabitants. He wished he could take Becky
to see it but doubted if she would be willing to venture so far into

the desert. Never the less he would ask her to go with him when she returned from school.

Ben arrived home a couple of days before Becky. Will was surprised at Ben's newfound maturity and poise. He had also become quite handsome, and outgoing. This was not lost on Helen who wasted no time in pointing out to Will and Nathan that they could learn a few things from Ben. Of course this had the opposite effect on them, and they determined to make her pay for drawing comparisons. They began at suppertime.

"Why did you give Ben the biggest steak?" asked Will. "What?" asked an astonished Helen. "I said, why did you give Ben the biggest steak?" Helen just looked at him, embarrassment flooding over her. Getting no answer Will continued, "First it was Nathan with the pie, then my chair, now it's the steak." Will was truly enjoying himself; So much so that he failed to note the anger that was building up in his mother. During the course of the meal Will spilled the gravy reaching for a slice of bread, and timing it just right, got the last piece of meat as Nathan was reaching for it. These were accompanied with other minor infractions of etiquette.

For his part Nathan kept up a one sided dialogue not giving anyone else a chance to talk. The final straw came when Nathan said, "Well Helen this wasn't the best meal you ever made but I guess it will do."

This was all Helen could handle. Grabbing a broom, she drove the men from her kitchen. With each swing she listed an offense. "I worked my fingers to the bone getting a nice supper and you complained about the meat when it was me who got stuck with the smallest piece. And as for you she shrieked at Nathan, talk, talk, talk. Don't you ever shut up? Can't you control yourself or your blooming' son? There is no excuse for raising your voice! It's just a good thing one of us can control herself or this place wouldn't be fit to live in."

By this time all three men were in a state of total helplessness, overcome with laughter. It was all put into perspective when Nathan said, "You're right dear from now on we will try to follow your example." Helen stood rooted to the floor, broom poised to strike again. "After all", continued Nathan, "one should always use tact and poise when dealing with an unpleasant situation." With a mighty swing the broom sailed over Nathan's head and he suddenly found himself smothered by his wife who was joining in their laughter. In their mirth they failed to notice the puzzled faced boarders who had come to investigate the commotion, or the indignant cat and dog who had been roused from their evening nap.

After things had settled down Will leaned back in his chair with a stretch and a yawn and said, "Well folks, I hate to put an end to such a stimulating evening but tomorrow is a big day. My sweetheart is coming home."

Will woke up early the next morning in a cold sweat by a dream that was so vivid he wasn't sure for a minute or so that it was a dream. In the dream a stagecoach was being chased by bandits. As the driver tried to round a sharp bend it flipped over, spilling luggage and passengers onto the road. The bandits checked each passenger and not finding the one they were looking for yanked the coach door open. At this point Will became part of the dream, looking over their shoulders into the coach. To his horror he saw the broken body of Becky.

He lay in his bed unable to move except for the spasms of fear that traveled up and down his body. His thoughts began to race, bringing accusation after accusation. Becky was due to arrive on the stage that evening. How could he have been so foolish? What was he thinking of? Remorse and anger gripped his soul as he denounced himself. It was so clear now that he couldn't believe he hadn't thought of it before. What better way to get even with him than to steal Becky off the stage.

His thoughts finally galvanized into action. Within minutes he had saddled Chalky and was galloping off into the predawn darkness. He would do all he could to make sure his nightmare didn't come true. He rode hard for five hours before finally admitting he must stop and find food for himself and Cisco. In his haste he had not bothered to pack anything but his gun. Fortunately he did have money in his pocket, but being some distance from a town he would have to trust himself to the hospitality of the next home he came to. As luck would have it he found a family just sitting down to breakfast and only too happy to share what they had with Will.

An hour later, having fed and rested Chalky, Will was once again on his way. Now he had a full canteen and a saddlebag filled with food, thanks to the kindness of the family who had fed him. Will determined that his and Becky's home would be the same. The thought of Becky once again filled him with anxiety and he had to check his impulse to rush headlong to her rescue. He realized that if someone was waiting for the stage he could blunder into their trap if he was not careful.

As he rode he tried to put himself in the shoes of the bandits. Suddenly he remembered a spot where the road narrowed leaving only enough room for a stage to squeeze between two rock out-croppings. They would be moving slow and Will was sure this was where they would try to stop it. After considering his options Will decided he had no choice but to cut across country. He had a good idea when the stage would pass that spot and realized he had time to make it if they traveled fast.

Two hours later a tired horse and rider eased themselves to the top of a rise and stopped. Off to the west some three miles away was the approaching stagecoach, and just two hundred yards below Will's vantage point were the three Dillon's, hidden right where he thought they would be. Knowing he must hurry, he carefully backed Chalky to where they were below the line of sight of the Dillons, then he quietly and quickly made his way to the road. Turning west he urged Chalky to a run in order to intercept the stage as far away from the Dillon's as possible. Fortunately the driver had stopped to rest the horses just as Will had gotten to the road so they were still nearly three miles from the Dillon's when Will intercepted them.

There were six people in the coach including the driver and guard, Becky, a middle aged woman and two men in their thirties, who looked like they could handle a gun. Will explained the situa-tion to them and suggested a plan. They all knew the Dillon's repu-tation and were eager to lend their help.

Meanwhile the Dillons were getting restless. The stage should have appeared by now. They began to argue with one another. Thad wanted to stay put a while longer, but wade and Todd wanted to go search for the stage. Thad finally gave in and they started down the road. They hadn't gone far before Thad suddenly reigned his horse "Shhhh. I said be quiet ya numskulls!" They sat quietly listening. "It sounds like music."

"Na, there ain't no music out here."

Thad took off his hat and swatted Todd a couple times across the side of his head. "I said be quiet! Get off your horses and follow me."

With that they began leading their horses toward the music. As they got closer they could hear a fiddle and a female voice, though they couldn't make out the words. Suddenly they rounded a little bend and no more then fifty yards ahead was a man playing his fiddle and a robust middle aged woman dancing to his music and singing at the top of her lungs. The two Dillon boys grinned at each other and began walking toward the pair. "Hold it." cautioned Thad "this may be some sort of trick."

By now the two boys were curious and in the mood to have some fun with the couple. Thad reluctantly followed his sons, keeping his hand on his gun, ready to use it the first sign of trouble. They were able to walk right up to the pair before they seemed to notice them.

"Hello boys, you're just in time to join our party!" "What kind of party?" asked Todd. "Why it's a necktie party" sang the women's voice as three loops sailed through the air and settled around their necks. They were immediately jerked off their feet, their curiosity being quickly replaced by a mixture of fear and rage. Each time one of them attempted to stand up, his rope was given a sharp jerk that caused it to dig into his neck. After several futile attempts to stand, they sullenly sat while their hands were being tied behind their backs. Then the stage was brought out of its hiding place and the end of each rope was attached to it.

The Dillon's had been totally surprised. It turned out that the little group of passengers was actually a troop of entertainers on their way to Yuma. They were more than happy to join the fun. All Will had to do was hide the coach and be ready with the driver and shotgun guard, to throw their lassoes.

"I hope you fellows can run as fast as these horses."

The sound of Will's voice stirred Thad out of his stupor. "Your going to pay for this Carter, you have no call to treat us this way."

"What about robbery and kidnapping?"

"Who did I rob and who did I kidnap?" retorted Thad.

Will exchanged glances with the driver. Dillon was right.

While there was no doubt in his mind what they were up to, there was absolutely no evidence to prove it. For their own safety they were forced to haul them back to Yuma where they released them on the outskirts of town.

Will didn't regret what he had done. He had no choice but he had added heat to the coals of hate that smoldered within the Dillons and could someday flare into murder.

Chapter 11

THE SUMMER WENT quickly for Will. It was good to have Ben and Becky home again and he made the most of the opportunity to be with them. He and Ben spent a lot of time at their swimming hole. He shared Ben's excitement over his schooling and listened with pleasure as Ben talked about his plans.

The three of them often took a picnic to the knoll overlooking the river. They had discovered a den of Foxes on the bank of the river and it was comical to watch the young twins frolic and run. To their great surprise Lucky made friends with them. Happy was indifferent and spent his time in the shade as Lucky stalked and pounced on the playful pair. They rolled and tumbled in the sand and chased each other until things got too rough for the cat, then he simply went up a tree. Will wondered what would happen if the mother found Lucky with her offspring but he seemed to know when it was time to leave.

It was not always trouble free for Will however. A shadow often hung over him. He missed Running Bird and he grieved over the loss of his friend Wayne. Mrs. Dillon was crushed by the death of her son and seemed to need to talk to Will about it. She had fled her home and moved into the boarding house. Helen also spent many hours with her as she struggled with grief for Wayne and fear of her husband. She also felt responsible for exposing the Penny's to danger. Will assured her that his troubles with Thad Dillon didn't have anything to do with her.

Toward the end of summer Becky found herself acting as a nurse to Lucky who discovered the hard way he wasn't a dog. It happened the day he innocently approached several dogs and nearly lost his life. He somehow escaped them and made his way home more dead than alive. Along with the wounds to his flesh was the loss of his carefree and trusting spirit; Indeed he even found it difficult to trust Happy for some time. It was only Becky's kind care that pulled him through. Becky was relieved when he finally returned to his habit of curling up with Happy at night. It was then she knew he would live.

Becky's compassion and kind spirit did not escape the attention of Will. His love for her deepened each day as more and more, her nature became evident, as did the inner conviction that they would share their future together helping others.

One day Will brought home a horse for Becky. She was small and dainty but very strong and quick. Her name was Midnight, an appropriate name for she was jet black. Becky thought she was the most beautiful horse she had ever seen and a bond quickly developed between them, much to Will's satisfaction. Each day after supper they rode out into the desert together. Will wanted to improve Midnight's stamina and Becky's riding skill. He also wanted Becky to become comfortable in the desert.

During these rides he told her about his adventures in the desert and the lessons he had learned. He also taught her how to find water by following game trails or footprints, and how to read the sky for signs of dangerous weather. Once they followed a set of tracks for a couple of miles to where a rider had set up camp. Will pointed out the signs that indicated he had spent several days there. It was then it dawned on him that he had probably been watching him and Becky.

Becky had a keen eye and a curious mind, often noticing things before Will did. She was also beginning to view the desert and it's inhabitants as friends, or as in the case of some of the less likable creatures such as snakes and spiders, at least as objects of interest. One evening she and Will were sitting on a big rock when she spied the biggest wasp she had ever seen. Her startled gasp brought Will back from his serene daydream and he almost fell off the rock. "Look for the Tarantula," he said. "What did you say?" she answered.

Will explained about the female Tarantula Hawk and it's method of providing food for her offspring. "Look...over there under that Creosote bush."

For the next half-hour they watched as the wasp stalked, and in a life and death struggle, finally killed the spider which was many times her size. She then buried it after depositing several eggs deep within it's bosom.

Will explained, "when the eggs hatch the young Wasps will feed on the spiders flesh until they are mature enough to survive on their own."

Becky smiled at Will and snuggled against his side. "I'm so lucky to have someone like you. I'm never afraid when you are with me." It was a little disturbing to realize Becky was sometimes fearful and that she put so much faith in him. His heart felt like it would burst with love as he looked into her trusting eyes and confessed his inability to provide the care and protection she deserved by himself. "The one who brought us together and is guiding us, will also enable us to be the partners both of us need." He knew she understood and agreed as she put her hand in his.

Once again their attention was diverted as they idly watched a pair of birds swoop and dive at a crow that had gotten too close to their nest. They took turns attacking from different directions, each time forcing the indignant thief to twist and roll, changing its direction. "He even teaches the little birds to care for one another and how to work together."

As they watched Becky began to reminisce. Will smiled to himself as she remembered aloud some of the good times they had enjoyed. Then she stopped for a moment and with a serious look on her face asked, "Why was Sweetheart not named after the markings on his forehead like Diamond was? After all Star seems much more appropriate for him than Sweetheart?" Will caught the twinkle in her eyes and knew she knew the truth and that he was in for some teasing about what she called his 'periodic breakdowns'. He smiled sheepishly as she recalled some of his past antics, and soon joined in with her gentle laughter. She reached over and took his hand again and Will's world was perfect.

Will would have been satisfied to live this moment forever but he knew it was not possible. He and Becky had decided she should return to teachers college for another term and it would soon be time for her to leave. He knew such moments, as this would be few and far between for a while. As if to punctuate the point Will spotted a horse and rider approaching.

Becky saw the concern on Will's face as he quickly scanned the countryside in every direction to be sure the rider wasn't seeking to distract him so others could catch him by surprise. As the rider drew closer he began to look familiar to Will but he was unable to place him until he raised his arm in greeting and put his horse to a run. "Well I'll be ...if it isn't Stone Walker...I wonder what he's doing way out here."

Stone stepped down from his horse and the two friends shook hands warmly. After a short conversation with Will he Turned to Becky and said, "Hi Becky My name is Stone, Now I understand why Will couldn't stop talking about you." Becky turned red and shook hands with him but didn't say anything.

As they rode toward home Stone explained that his grandfather, Silver Hair, had sent him to ask Will to come for a visit. There were things about to happen that could spell disaster for the residents of the Valley of refuge. The arrival of the railroad in Yuma, and the passage of the Desert Land act by the United States Congress would open the flood gates and create an onslaught that the Indian people would be helpless to stand against.

Stone waited until the next morning at breakfast, when everyone was present, to explain in detail. As they sat drinking coffee he outlined the implications for the Indians. The arrival of the railroad would bring a major influx of people. With relatively inexpensive transportation and easy access to markets farming and ranching would be more profitable. Of course this would mean land would be in greater demand and no place would be safe.

The Desert Land Act would make it virtually impossible for the Indians to keep the land they had because it opened vast tracts for homesteading, including the Indian land. At the same time Indians were not eligible to homestead.

"So once again the United States Government has passed a law that makes it legal to steal what rightly belongs to other men." Stone's face was grim as his eyes swept his shamefaced friends, and he continued. "I blame none of you for I know you are good people. That is why I am here asking for your help." Silver Hair had a plan to save his valley that involved Will and his family. Stone asked Nathan and Helen as well as Becky and the Cully's to join him and Will. Will was quite surprised to learn that Stone and the Cully's were good friends. Indeed, Dr. Cully was quite familiar with the valley and it's residents, having known Silver Hair for several years, and had spent time regularly in the valley giving medical treatment when needed.

Becky and the Cully's agreed to go with Stone, as did Nathan and Ben, but Helen excused herself because of her 'medical condition'.

Will responded with irritation. "What medical condition? You look just fine to me."

Helen smiled at him and patted his arm. "You're going to be a big brother." Will sat with a blank look on his face, seeming not to comprehend his mother's words. Finally she said "I'm going to have a baby."

Still saying nothing, Will looked from face to face until his eyes fell on Nathan then he mumbled "well, I'll be."

The room instantly came alive as Becky and Rose excitedly began to chatter away with Helen about things that didn't interest the men. Stone sipped his coffee while saying good-by to his hopes for an early start back to the valley. To his great surprise they did get on the road by mid morning. They planned to go easy and take two or three days. This was partly in consideration for Dr. Cully who had never completely recovered from his appendix attack.

All went well until the morning of the third day when Will, who had been checking their back-trail, rode into camp to announce that they were being followed by three riders. Stone got busy immediately laying the fuel for two fires, one quite large and the other, somewhat smaller, about fifty feet away and in the direction he intended to travel. He lit the large one first, and using his horse blanket sent up three puffs of smoke. Then he ran and lit the other fire and sent up a continuous line of smoke. After putting the fires out he sat scanning the horizon until he spotted a line of smoke so thin and far away that no one else would have noticed it. After a quick breakfast they got under way. Stone began to change course, but did it gradually so their followers wouldn't notice.

They had been travelling some time and it was late afternoon when they entered a narrow canyon. Stone commented that it only had one way in and one way out. "Our travelling companions will be dealt with here and sent on their way", he said.

The Dillon boys were tired and fed up with the heat and dust. They were also out of patience with their father, who had a habit of taking out his frustration on whoever was closest to him. Todd and Wade had been the targets of his abuse for the last several days, having endured cuffs to the side of the head and boots to the seat of the pants, as well as a constant stream of verbal abuse. They had followed Will's party into the canyon and Wade was uneasy about it. He kept checking their back trail feeling they were being followed and each time he did he got a tongue lashing from Thad Dillon.

Finally fed up, he drew his horse to a stop and took a drink from his canteen. He sat watching as Thad and Todd slowly drew away from him. He wasn't going to put up with any more, nor was he going to eat any more dust. He would follow at a comfortable distance. It didn't take long for Thad to notice and respond. "Hey, you lazy numskull, get up here where you belong."

"I think I'll ride along behind where it's more pleasant." Wade answered. "In a pig's eye you will", shouted Thad, "You get up here now or else I'm going to put a knot on that ugly head of yours!"

That was the last straw. Wade spurred his horse to a run and headed straight for his dad who sat with a smirk on his face. It was wiped away quickly as Wade closed the distance between them at full speed. As he swept by his fist shot out catching Thad on the chin, sending him off his horse in a backward summersault into a cactus patch where he lay out cold.

Todd and Wayne stared at each other for a moment then they realised they need not let fear of their father control them any longer. Their relief coupled with the comical manner in which Thad had dismounted his horse resulted in laughter, which welled up from their innermost being; something they hadn't experienced for a long time.

They sat enjoying the release until it began to dawn on them that there was something wrong. There were too many people laughing. It should only be the two of them. They looked over at their father but he was just beginning to stir. Then they saw several mounted Indian braves surrounding them, and each one was laughing. They had witnessed the scene and had found it as humorous also.

Thad came too and he was seething with anger. Not yet aware of the spot he was in, he bellowed, "Who knocked me off my horse?"

Wade replied, "Why Pa, one of these Indians knocked you clean off your horse." Thad looked at Todd with a questioning eye.

"That's right Pa", he lied, "It was one of these Indians."

It began to dawn him that he and his sons were in a spot. He looked from one brave to another trying to discern which one might be the leader and what frame of mind they were in. At this point they all looked pretty serious. They sat looking at each other for what seemed like an eternity, then one of the brave's spoke. "I am Red Fox. Why did you come into our sacred canyon? No white man has ever come here and left alive." Thad began to sweat, unable to speak in his own defense, so overcome by fear that words wouldn't come.

He and his sons sat helplessly as the Indians began to shout abuses at them. From time to time one of them would begin to approach the captives but Red Fox would call him back. Then they started discussing amongst themselves what they were going to do the captives. As they sat and listened to the imaginative options being suggested they became weak with fear. They didn't notice the smiles which crossed the faces of the braves therefore they were unaware that the whole discussion was for their benefit.

Finally after much arguing and shouting they tied their captives up, and building a fire, curled up and went to sleep. It was a long and bitter night for the Dillon's. They had neither the warmth of a blanket or the ability to get comfortable, bound up with rope as they were. It was with mixed feelings that they watched the sun come up. They were thankful for the end of a sleepless night but fearful that they might never see the new day through.

They were relieved of their boots and camping gear, Then the Indians began looking their horses over and arguing amongst themselves about them. Finally, at a word from Red Fox, two braves left taking the horses with them.

Thad was furious but he kept quiet realizing that he and his son's were at the mercy of their captors. Taking his bow, Red Fox pointed in the direction they should start walking. He told them their way would be plainly marked and warned them to follow the signs or suffer the consequences. "Go now before the sun makes the sand too hot for your bare feet." With that they were sent on their way.

They walked about a quarter of a mile before they spotted their boots, then it was two miles to where their horses were tied. By that time their feet were hot and blistered but they were so relieved and grateful for the horses that they didn't complain. After travelling several hours, following the course marked out for them, they came upon their gear laid out in a camp all set up for them.

The next day they made it back to their hide out. Thad Dillon was more determined than ever to discover the location of the Indian village. Though he was unaware of the beauty and true potential for wealth it represented, he did understand there was something in the desert well worth persuing. He was unaware of the number of people ready to defend the valley with their lives.

Chapter 12

BECKY COULDN'T BELIEVE her eyes as she rode into the valley. The contrast between the dry barren landscape of the desert and the lush green trees and cultivated fields of this protected little world was nothing short of miraculous to her. Where just moments ago there had been dust devils there was now the fragrance of orange blossoms and the warm soft air had a pleasing moistness to it that caressed one's skin rather than drying it out as the desert air did.

Looking across the valley she spied a doe with her newborn fawn resting in the luxurious ferny grass under some trees. They displayed no fear as a small herd of sheep led by a young Indian boy trespassed upon their haven and began to graze. The fawn apparently thinking he was a sheep joined the lambs in their leaping and running. He came to an abrupt stop however, when he found himself face to face with the young shepherd. Feeling a vague sense of discomfort the doe called for her fawn and led him to a safer spot not far away.

It wasn't long before Becky and her party were surrounded by a group of smiling, laughing children. As they neared the center of the village Teresa ran up and embraced Will. At first Becky was jealous but as she looked into Terisa's eyes she saw the love of a girl for a brother or protector. She saw mutual respect between the two; respect born of a solitude shared in the desert when they fought side by side against common enemies who wanted to destroy them. She had no difficulty responding to the warm embrace she received when introduced to Terisa.

The rest of the afternoon and evening was spent in eating and getting to know one another. Later on after most of the children had gone to bed several adults remained by the fire. It was story time. One by one, beginning with the youngest they began to tell their stories. There were only two rules, each teller must be invited to tell his story and the story must be true.

Terisa was asked to tell of her rescue by Will. She left out nothing. Becky sat leaning against Will's side listening with pride and filled with gratitude. She saw clearly what a man of honor and integrity he was and wondered why she was so blessed to be loved by him. She determined in her heart that she would never take him for granted.

Then Becky was asked to tell how she and Will met. Will blushed and the people roared with laughter as she told how he walked into the horse and the terrible time he had at supper with his rebellious fork. She left nothing out except the part about "Sweetheart." She also confessed how her heart had leaped inside her when she first laid eyes on him.

Finally it was time for one more story. A young brave sitting back out of the light of the fire began to tell how he had seen Terisa and fallen in love with her. As he told about his efforts to win her his voice cracked from time to time almost as if he was afraid to allow himself to be heard. He hesitated briefly, then continued, "My story really goes back further," and he began to speak in generalities, as if hesitating to give information that might reveal too much.

He spoke of a searching heart that took him many places and of questions he could not find answers for until he finally realized that there is one Creator who created men of every race and who had one Son who shows the way to everyone who will follow. He finally realized this Creator was not just the White man's Creator.

Then he paused and gathered himself and continued. "Through all my wandering and questioning there was one person I knew I could always count on. The answers he gave me were always with me. He will always be my greatest friend." With that he stood up and with a voice no longer masked said "Thank you Will, you are a true friend."

Will sat in stunned silence. Running Bird stood before him, hand outstretched waiting to greet him. Will struggled to his feet and stepped toward his friend, unable to see him through the tears that filled his eyes. The two men were unaware of the others who began slipping slowly away from the fire. They stood embracing for several minutes, until Nathan and Ben spoke to Running Bird. After expressing their gladness to see him they also left. Then Will noticed Becky and Terisa standing nearby. Becky was overcome and weeping but Terisa was beaming and for the first time Will heard her deep throated laugh.

They sat by the fire for several hours talking. Running Bird told in detail about his search, and he and Terisa told about their chance meeting shortly after Will had left the Valley. Running Bird had studied about irrigation and water management and Stone had persuaded him to come to the Valley to help. It was with a sense of deep satisfaction and anticipation that Will finally fell asleep in the early morning hours.

The next day was busy. Becky, Rose, and Dr. Cully were given a tour of the village. Wherever they went they were warmly welcomed. Will, Ben, Nathan, and Running Bird went with Stone and Silver Hair. They first went to the foot of twin Eagle peaks where Running Bird explained his plan to split the spring and divert half it's volume so that each side of the valley had plenty of water. Then they climbed up the East peak until they reached a spot where mining was obviously taking place. Stone handed Nathan a sample of ore. Nathan couldn't believe his eyes, for in his hand was the richest sample that he had ever seen.

In the afternoon Silver Hair produced a rough map of the Valley and the area surrounding it, then he proceeded to explain his plan. Will and Nathan would file a claim that covered the mine and surrounding land. Then they would take Stone and Silver Hair as partners.

Silver Hair had the valley staked according to the Desert Land Act. Will, Ben, Nathan, Dr. Cully, Becky, and Rose would each file a homestead claim. By doing this and meeting the homestead requirements they would guarantee control of the Valley. Stone already had the necessary papers made out so all they had to do was sign them and make sure they were filed properly.

Will and Nathan were deeply touched by the total trust Silver Hair was demonstrating. Will also knew it would mean work and sacrifice on the part of each one to fulfil the law. Each homestead must have a dwelling built on it and there must be improvements made each year.

That evening Will and Nathan explained the plan to the rest. Each one must decide what to do. Will was not too surprised when every one said yes. The only stipulation was that they all work together. Of course Ben and Becky would be away at school and would be able to actually live on their claim a few months of the year so most of the actual building would have to be done for them. Later that evening Becky and Will walked out to their homestead sites. They were side by side and totaled three hundred and twenty acres. They walked up toward the East Peak until they came to an ideal building site. Protected in the back by a rock cliff some two hundred feet high and sheltered by a forest of trees it never the less presented an unrestricted view of the entire valley. Becky and Will stood hand in hand. This was where they would build their home and where they intended to build their future. They didn't need to talk about it for they knew in their hearts they had been brought to this place together for a purpose.

Within a few days, preparations were completed and it was time to put the plan into action. Will and Nathan would go to Prescott with Stone to file the mine claim and the homestead papers. With the futures of so many at stake it was felt the papers should be filed in person. In the past, too many claims had disappeared in the mail to suit Nathan.

Two parties left under cover of darkness. One was headed north to Prescott. The other headed for Yuma. An escort of Indians accompanied Ben, Dr. Cully, Becky and Rose. Riders had been seen several times, obviously searching for the valley, so the villagers took no chances with the well being of their friends. They had also stationed more lookouts to guard the approaches and organized the villagers so that each person knew his duty and his post if the village was attacked.

Chapter 13

MEAN WHILE THAD Dillon had had not been idle. While all the plans had been made and set into motion in the Valley he had been making his own plans. For starters he realized that he needed more help. He had also figured out what Will was up to. This was partially due to one of the villagers who had strayed from his post and met up with some of Thad's men. One of them recognized him and knew of his past problem with alcohol. Through a combination of intimidation and feigned friendship they soon had the brave drunk to the point where he told all he knew. Then they simply dumped him in the desert confident he wouldn't remember a thing the next morning.

Thad realized he must prevent Will from filing the claims and had actually gotten a head start on him. He, along with his sons and three others was waiting to ambush Will and his party. Will felt confident that they had gotten away without being observed never the less he kept a wary eye out as they rode. His diligence was rewarded soon enough when he suddenly caught the flash of sunlight off in the distance. It had to be a rifle barrel or some other piece of metal. Will immediately reigned Chalky to a stop and began checking his hooves.

"We have company ahead," said Will. "You can bet if they know where we're headed they also know about the claims," added Nathan.

"Follow Me," said Stone, "I think I know a place where we can give them the slip."

They turned their horses and slipped behind a small swell that blocked them from sight of Thad and his dry gulchers. Keeping to low ground they entered a protected area where they stopped for a rest. They had to act soon. The Dillon gang would be coming after them before long. Their options were limited. They either must fight or attempt to loose them. Neither option held much promise.

"How about a strategic retreat?" suggested Stone. "We'll make them think there are three of us. One of us will lay back and every time they get a little close we'll kick some gravel in their faces. Will was against it but Stone and Nathan insisted that he make a run for Prescott. Stone drew a rough map showing Will the best way then sent him on the ride of his life.

Things went bad from the beginning. Thad had wasted no time in locating the spot where they had hidden and had seen Will leave. He hurried back to where his gang was waiting and instructed them to let Stone and Nathan lead them wherever they choose. He and his sons would take care of Will once and for all.

Will was not aware he was riding into an ambush. It had been a long day and he was tired. A false sense of security allowed him to relax and he was soon dozing as Chalky followed an old path toward their destination. Some four hundred yards away three sets of eyes watched him approach. Thad fidgeted nervously seeking to quell the eagerness rising up inside. He had told his sons to hold their fire. Will belonged to him.

Both of them were relieved. Their hatred for Will had slowly diminished over time and had been replaced by a growing respect. He had beaten them fair and square every time they had challenged him and each time he had refused to get even or press his advantage. Instead he had allowed them to walk away. They had never discussed their feelings and both felt alone. They were filled with guilt but the fear they held for their father kept them from interfering with him as he lined up his sights on Wills chest.

Providence is not limited by time or by odds. As each second ticked off, Will's odds for survival diminished. Thad was waiting for the shot that couldn't miss and his target was getting bigger by the moment. Finally with a gleam in his eye he sucked in his breath, exhaled briefly, then held it. As the rifle steadied he squeezed the trigger. Almost simultaneously with the rifles report Wills head snapped forward and his body folded throwing him off the saddle. His foot caught in the stirrup as Chalky bolted. Will's limp body rolled and flopped as it struck stones and shrubs. Chalky veered to the left and fled into a ravine where he finally came to a stop.

Thad was beside himself with joy. He kept pacing back and forth congratulating himself. Todd and Wade were heartsick. To kill in a fair fight was one thing but to dry-gulch a man was another. At that very moment they both determined to have nothing more to do with Thad Dillon or his ways.

Unaware of his sons feelings he instructed them to go make sure Will was dead and take any papers they found on him. As they rode away he reached into his saddlebag and brought out a bottle of whiskey. Wade nodded with satisfaction. The whiskey would make his leaving all the easier.

Meanwhile Chalky had trotted a hundred yards farther up the ravine then came to another stop. He turned his head and looked down at Will and pawed the ground nervously as the smell of blood filled his nostrils. He was about to flee when a soft groan stopped him. Will's body trembled and shook from head to toe briefly then it lay motionless. After several minutes it jerked and gave a rattling cough. Then one eye opened for a brief moment. Suddenly both eyes shot open as Will became conscious.

He tried in vain to remember what had happened. It was several minutes before he could speak. "Well Chalky, I guess I fell asleep." Then he noticed the blood and the painful crease in his side. At the moment when Thad pulled the trigger, Chalky had stepped into a hole causing Will's head to snap forward and his body to fold. Instead of destroying Will's heart the bullet had creased his side.

The realization that he had been shot made him break out in a cold sweat. He realized he was in grave danger as his enemy would surely come looking for him. After a couple of attempts he was able to stand beside his horse. He washed his wound and put a handkerchief on it and prepared to mount Chalky.

The sound of approaching horses stopped him. He quickly backed Chalky and himself into a clump of brush and drawing his gun, waited.

Wade and Todd were not prepared to meet Will this way. They were positive he was dead, having seen his body convulse when hit by their father's bullet. They were both angry. They were angry with their father for his insistence that Will be killed, and they were angry at themselves for not stopping him.

The sound of his voice caused them to freeze. He stood ready for a gunfight, expecting the worst, but the look on their faces totally confused him. It was one of surprise then relief.

"Don't shoot, we don't want to fight any more." Wade's words were confirmed by uplifted hands. Will could only look at his long time foes in wonder as Wade continued.

"I'm tired of the hatred and revenge, and killing and I want no more of it." Without thought Wade reached toward Will to offer his hand in reconciliation, forgetting that Will's right hand was holding a gun. Will jerked back instinctively.

Wade saw his mistake at once and his hands went back up. He attempted to explain but was so distraught he could only stand red faced. Todd came to his rescue. "Please give us a chance to explain Will, I don't blame you if you kill us but please let us explain."

Will hesitated a moment. "throw your guns over by that tree and be very careful about it." The brothers complied instantly then they began to tell their story. They both had become sick and tired of the life their father had led them into but they were afraid to cross him. That is until today when he ambushed Will.

"We just want to ride away and start over again." "How do I know your not lying?" asked Will.

"I don't blame you for not believing us but I will tell you this, there are three men trying to kill Nathan and the Indian. There are also more than forty five ready to attack the hidden village as soon as Pa is sure you have been 'taken care of' as he puts it." Will holstered his gun as Wade continued. "The best thing for you to do is to get those papers filed as soon as possible and get back to warn your friends."

"Where is Thad?" asked Will.

"He's on the other side of that ridge and by this time-dead drunk. We'll go find him and tell him we found a pool of blood but your horse drug you off. Then I'm hitting the trail."

Todd dressed Will's wound and bound it up so it wouldn't start bleeding. Wade stood by obviously feeling awkward. He wanted to make amends but didn't know how. "I know we will never be friends but I", his words failing him, Wade once again offered Will his hand. After a brief handshake they parted ways. Will realized he had a lot of ground to cover. He was tempted to go back at once but knew he must get the papers properly recorded.

He pushed as hard as he and Chalky could bear and arrived in Prescott late in the evening, where he was surprised to find the land titles office still open. The clerk explained that ever since the Desert Land Act had become law there had been more claims than could be handled during regular hours. Will got Chalky to the livery stable and after a good super was glad to find a hotel were he was soon sound asleep.

He left early the next morning aware that he had a good sixty miles to cover before he reached his friends. He carried a knot in his stomach, caused by worry over what had become of Stone and Nathan and what he would find at the Valley of Refuge.

All was quiet when he arrived at the place he had left Nathan and Stone. Will traveled carefully, following their tracks. He was soon able to tell what happened by the signs left in the sand. After playing cat and mouse for several miles they had simply out run their pursuers and headed for the valley. Will knew Thad would be there with close to fifty men with only one aim, which was to get possession of the valley regardless of the cost.

It was still dark when Will and Chalky, both exhausted, approached the hidden entrance to the valley. The glow and presence of smoke from several campfires told him that the village was surrounded. They were forced to go slow and careful. Any sound could be fatal. They were finally able to slip through the entrance without being seen or heard. The next trick was to keep from being killed by one of the guards protecting the valley. They made it through the guards just before sunrise.

Will was relieved when the Eastern sky began to lighten. He walked to his homestead site in order to get a good view of the situation. As daylight chased the shadows away he was relieved to see

Nathan approaching. He quickly explained the situation. Dillon had attacked around noon the day before with close to fifty men. The defenders had been positioned well and had turned them back each time they tried to break through. Just before sundown Thad had approached under a white flag and announced that he had sent for reinforcements. A train loaded with about a hundred homesteaders had arrived in Yuma and they were eager to help throw the Indians off their land.

Thad had also announced that Will was dead and that the law was behind the homesteaders. Silver Hair called Thad a liar and gave him thirty seconds to get behind cover. After that there was only scattered fighting. As Nathan finished, Stone and Silver Hair arrived. They were overjoyed to see Will and breathed a sigh of relief when told that all the claims had been recorded. Thad Dillon had nothing to stand on now that the land was legally homesteaded to qualified citizens of the United States.

Thad was awakened by a cheer coming from the village. Will's presence was announced by shouts of joy. Thad could only stare in disbelief as Will and Silver hair walked up to a high spot that could be seen by both groups. Before Thad could do anything, Will announced that the claims were all recorded. He suggested that the attackers go look for land someplace else.

Tired and disgruntled, several of them began to pack up and leave. Thad was infuriated and began to shout abuses to Will and the Indians. This was his undoing. As he ranted and raved he revealed his duplicity. The men who still remained realized that they had been used and lied to and soon Thad Dillon's army melted away. He rode away cursing Will and reciting the things he was going to do to get even.

As for Will he was eager to get to work fulfilling the dreams of so many people. It was especially hard leaving Becky in San Diego for another year but they both knew it was for the best. She needed as much training as possible because she would be running Twin Eagles school.

Chapter 14

WILL'S DREAM FOR the people of the Valley would touch every aspect of their lives. He was not of the opinion that the Indians needed their lives planned out for them as so many White people believed. He did feel that the White man was taking their land and with it the possibility to hunt or grow their own food. They were also, even now in the process of destroying the Indians way of life and sense of identity. Will believed the White man had a moral obligation to provide a way for them to rebuild their lives and futures.

Will had a list of some basic needs that he intended to be provided. This included Employment, with an opportunity to choose and advance according to interest and ability; Education; Medical care and Spiritual care. The Valley community was being set up to enable the residents to provide these things for themselves.

The mine was rich and promised many years of productivity. This would provide funds for a school and medical clinic. Other spin-offs would include a general store, a blacksmith, a church, and agricultural enterprises as varied as the imagination of those involved.

Will worked hard and the time went fast. After building the required dwellings for himself and Becky's homesteads he began working on their permanent home. He ordered timbers and lumber and gathered tons of granite stones that had been created by Running Birds diversion of the spring as he blasted a passageway through several feet of rock.

Will and Becky had spent many happy hours planning their home of the future; never thinking it would become a reality so soon. The events that unfolded beginning with the rescue of Terisa, while a Godsend for Silver hair and his people had also created a great opportunity for Will. He saw it as much more, however, than just an opportunity. The ideas and dreams that began as tiny seeds in Will's heart were becoming in reality far more than what he had imagined. Just as a small seed if planted and watered can grow into a tall oak and give testimony to the life giving capability of water, so the efforts of man when nurtured and guided by providence can accomplish things far beyond his dreams or expectations.

Each day as his house came closer to completion, Will was reminded that he and Becky were part of a plan that went far beyond themselves and would continue long after they were gone.

The house was basic in design. The front door entered into a large living room, which was separated from the dinning room by a stone fireplace. The kitchen opened to both rooms. The effect was that of three separate rooms but one large space. There was also a den and pantry as well as a staircase leading to the upper floor which was divided into four bedrooms.

The combination of stone and mortar walls with large windows and the cedar shake roof supported with large beams, made the house not only strong but also beautiful to look at. Will built a veranda on three sides of the house which he hoped would provide for many hours of enjoyment gazing at the beautiful valley and visiting with friends

Will had other responsibilities besides completing his house. He spent several hours each day at the mine. He hired several of the villagers to farm his and Becky's land. This provided employment to those who had been farming it for several years. Their wages consisted of the crop they took off the land. Will was careful to do personally all that was required to fulfil the homestead conditions.

Nathan was just as busy, dividing his time between the mine and building their new home. He also spent time in Yuma where Helen was waiting for the arrival of their child. The boarding house was being taken over by Mrs. Dillon. Helen was anxious to see her new home and anticipated the day when she and her new baby could move in.

Rose and Dr. Cully had to hire help to build their homes. Because of their involvement in setting up the clinic and Dr. Cully's past service to the village Silver Hair put them on a regular salary. Rose was strong and anticipated spending several years with Twin Eagles Enterprises. Dr. Cully was getting frail and was unable to do heavy work but his wisdom and guidance were invaluable.

So the year went. Each one involved did his share and more. Stone directed and coordinated each of the businesses and services. By the end of the year all of them were running or, as in the case of the school, ready to open in the fall.

≫ ≪

It was a beautiful evening. Will and Helen were sitting on Will's veranda enjoying the view. They had just returned from supper and Will was holding his little brother Tom on his lap, marveling at the love he had for him. He thought of the possibility of having a son of his own and tears came to his eyes. They were tears of joy and anticipation at the thought of his little brother some day running and playing with his own son.

Suddenly a hint of a smile drifted across Will's face then vanished as he stifled a laugh that was threatening to escape.

"Don't get started on that," admonished Helen. Will collected himself momentarily, then he gave in to the mirth he no longer could control. "It's time Helen" he choked out. The stern expression she had tried to hold on her face melted and her laughter lost itself in that of Will's.

Nathan was about to join them but he turned and walked away in disgust. He knew they were reliving the night of his son's birth.

Helen had been awake for some time trying to conquer her restlessness. Then the pains started and she knew it was time. She gently reached over and shook Nathan. "It's time dear." There was no response so she called him again. There was still no answer. The third time she spoke with authority. "Nathan, get up! It's time!" Nathan's eyes popped open and he looked around for a moment. Then he understood.

"It's time!" he shouted. "Helen, get up, it's time!" With that he was out the door. Will's door was the closest, and Nathan began pounding on it while shouting, "Wake up Will, it's time." From there Nathan rushed into Rose Cully's room, not considering she would rather he knocked first. Rose sat calmly while he made his announcement.

"Don't you think it would be appropriate to put on some pants Nathan?" Nathan looked down blankly then he went searching for his wife. He found Will and the Dr. in the kitchen. Rushing into the bedroom he found Helen sitting in her chair. "Helen, where have you been? Don't you know it's time?" Helen smiled at her husband.

"Try to settle down. It's all right. Everything is under control."

"Sure," he said "and I'll tell you one thing, if you don't start cooperating you won't be there in time, then how do you think you'll feel when you miss the birth of your own child?"

Will, his soul content, wiped the tears from his eyes. They were tears of laughter and of gratitude. He smiled over at his mother and they bowed their heads. "Thank you Lord," he prayed, "for such a little brother. And thank you for Nathan such a wonderful father."

Nathan rejoined them and they began to talk of the past several months. Much had happened and much was still to take place. Will gave a little shudder as a wave of fear mingled with anticipation washed over him. Saturday was his wedding day.

The Valley of refuge was known throughout the Territory of Arizona. Will still found it hard to believe that several hundred people had made it their home. There was no problem providing work. The mine and other businesses had prospered, as did the agriculture enterprises. For many the valley was a stop off and trading center. It was the source of hope and help for many Indians who otherwise would be living in despair. Will surveyed the scene before him then he lifted his eyes heavenward.

Nathan and Helen excused themselves leaving Will to ponder his good fortune alone. He felt blessed in so many ways. He was marrying a wonderful girl whom he loved very much. He had friends that he could count on. And he was part of an enterprise that was helping many people. All these added up to a great future. Will once again bowed his head in humble gratitude. "Lord, this is the fruit of your vision, Your power and love. You have planted a spring of water that gushes forth with refreshment and life to those who otherwise would perish in a parched and barren land. Thank you for letting me be a part of it"

Will was reminded of the words of Jesus to the woman he had spoken to at the well, long ago, who so desperately needed refreshing. "...Whoever drinks of the water that I shall give him shall never thirst; but the water that I shall give him shall become in him a well of water springing up to eternal life." (John 4:14 NASV)

Why, he wondered to himself, do people so often insist on going to dry wells. Will continued his prayer. "Lord may I always lead Becky to the genuine springs, the ones fed by your Spirit. May I always be a spring flowing with your living water. I give you my life again."

Chapter 15

WILL WOKE SLOWLY to his wedding day, surprised at the somber, foreboding feeling that hovered around him. He had expected to wake with a burst of joy that would carry him through the entire day. He rested his head back on the pillow and began

To search for an explanation and as he did things began to

Come into focus.

For starters Running Bird had paid him a surprise visit the night before. He had tried to sneak in through the window as he always did when he was a boy. This time his foot caught on the curtain and he fell with a thud on the floor. Will, who was sleeping leaped out of bed in a daze and landed on top of Running Bird. In his semi-conscious panic he began to strangle his friend. It was only the quick response of Helen Carter that saved him as she rushed into the room and rescued him from Will's clutches.

After things settled down they visited well into the wee hours of the night. The empty pie plates gave testimony of the good time they shared, and the depth of their friendship.

Will was also reminded that the wind had been terrible all night. He was relieved that there was good reason for the sad shape he was in, and the irritability began to leave him. He had grown somewhat irritable over the past few weeks. Nathan had been quick to notice and took every opportunity to add as much discomfort as possible. There wasn't much Will could say about it considering the way he had treated Nathan at his wedding time.

A smile flit across his face as his thoughts rested on their most resent disagreement. Will was planting a Chinese Elm tree and Nathan had advised him to move it closer to the river where it would get plenty of moisture. Will wanted it where he and Becky could see it from their veranda so he disregarded Nathan's advice.

"I suppose I better go check on that tree" mused Will as he pulled his pants and shoes on. Early on as a boy, Will had determined to benefit from the wisdom and guidance Nathan offered. Even in his youth he came to respect him for the value he placed upon Scripture and the guidance it provided.

To Will Nathan fit perfectly the description of a wise man, given in Psalm 1. "Blessed is the man. . .whose delight is in the Law of the Lord . . .he will be like a tree firmly planted by streams of water." (Psalm 1:1-3 paraphrased)

"You just can't ask for a better friend," he thought. Will wasn't surprised to find the little tree laying flat on the ground. It wasn't broken, but bent over. It was unable to withstand the wind; supple enough to bend but not strong enough to stand in adversity.

Just then Nathan happened by. "Nice tree you have there Will."

"Thanks," muttered Will. His eyes followed the retreating form of Nathan. He knew he was his best friend. True, Nathan was his father by adoption but he had been careful to build love and commitment into the relationship.

As he absently transplanted the little tree down by the river, Will's mind traced some of the friendships of Scripture, such as David and Jonathan; and Paul and Barnabas. It dawned on him that some of the great men of the Bible were known for their friendship with God. God talked face to face with Moses as one speaks to his friend. (Exodus 33:"11) Abraham was called a friend of God. (James 2:23)

Will remembered the statement by Terisa about his friendship with God. It made him uncomfortable because he felt unworthy of such a high position. At the same time it intrigued him. Was it really possible? Almost as if answering a call three verses of Scripture popped into his head, ".. Abraham believed God . . and he was called the friend of God." (James 2:23) "Greater love has no one but this, that one lay down his life for his friends." (John 14:13) "You are my friend if you do what I command you." (John 14:15). Will decided he would think on this matter again. Today he was entering into a new relationship with Becky that involved a total commitment of himself and his love. He also felt if he was to be a good husband he must be close to God; as close as possible.

Will decided to go and share his thoughts with Becky. Unfortunately, Helen met him at the door. She held the conviction that the groom should not see his bride until the ceremony began. To do so would bring bad luck. "You will have your entire life to tell her things. Just give her a little peace today." With that she gave him a hand full of cookies and gently closed the door in his face.

The day went quick enough and Will soon found himself at the church. His emotions were uncontrollable and had taken him on a ride from the hights of joy to the depths of misery. Now he was just plain nervous. He had a lump in his throat and a knot in his stomach. His skin was crawling with chills yet he was perspiring.

Pastor Tomkins gave him a sympathetic look and led him and his friends to their places in front of the congregation. Will was seized by panic as he tried to find a place to focus his eyes. A gentle cough and nudge from the pastor made him aware that his hands were in his pockets. He grinned and sheepishly removed them. Unfortunately they almost immediately found themselves in his back pockets. Will angrily yanked them out and was distressed to hear the ripping sound the pocket made as it separated from the seat of his pants.

Running Bird softly whispered a few words of encouragement and Will finally settled down, just in time for the processional to start. First came Rose Cully then came Terisa. Will's cheeks flushed when he got a glimpse of Becky with Dr. Cully. As the bridal march began Dr. Cully handed Becky a small package.

"Your Aunt Martha asked me to give this to you." Becky's eyes started to fill with tears as she recognized the little Bible bound in white calf's skin. It had belonged to her grandmother. Becky's mother had carried it in her wedding as did her Aunt Martha. Becky was filled with appreciation. She knew what a great sacrifice this was for her aunt. The doctor laid a Sego Lilly on top of the Bible and gently led Becky down the isle to present her to Will.

Will was almost overcome when he looked into Becky's beautiful eyes. They sparkled and danced, reflecting the love that filled her heart. He would have been hopelessly trapped, unable to tear himself away from they're captivating power had he not been distracted by the most wonderful smile he had ever seen. Becky's dress was simple in design but beautifully stitched by Helen. It was obvious that much love had gone into the dress. The result was a perfect fitting dress that suited her form and bearing.

Will was lost in the glory of the moment and Running Bird was forced to give him a solid nudge to bring him back to reality. Becky had arranged for a friend from San Diego to sing during the wedding ceremony. As she began it was obvious that there was going to be a problem. The boys were immediately taken back to the infamous music night, now known as the Myrtle Brown fiasco. Before he could think, Running Bird whispered "its Myrtle Brown come back to haunt us!" Four men including the Pastor entered into a life and death struggle. Each one knew he must not loose control. Though they shared a common goal the reasons that motivated them differed. For Will it was his love and consideration for Becky. He vowed that he would not tarnish the wedding ceremony and the memories of it. For Running Bird it was a matter of survival. Having been told the Myrtle Brown story Terisa was now saying with her eyes that there would be dire consequences if Running Bird gave in to laughter. He had learned early in his marriage that it was wise to heed what her eyes said.

Ben, though his insides were convulsing with his efforts to stifle the mirth, knew the hurt the soloist would experience. She was not all that sure of herself and to agree to sing at all was a big step in her life personally. As for Pastor Tomkins it was a matter of personal and professional prestige. His position simply would not allow it.

So the personal dramas worked themselves out and the battles were won. It was with an audible sigh that the Pastor thanked the girl and continued the wedding. Nathan leaned over and whispered into Helen's ear, "You know, I think Will is growing up." Helen squeezed his hand and said a little prayer of gratitude.

The rest of the ceremony went well. The Pastors devotional was on the theme of the importance of friendship in the marriage. Will marveled at the way the Pastor's thoughts coincided with his own thoughts that day. Following the exchanging of vows the Pastor asked for the ring. Ben reached over with it and it slipped from his hand. He made a stab at it only to send it about four feet into the air. Will saved the day by deftly reaching out at just the right instant and catching it then with a flourish he handed it to the Pastor.

The first person to greet the couple was Nathan. "Nice touch with the ring son." His hand shake revealed a slight tremble and Nathan's eyes misted as he said, "I am proud to be your Dad"

Chapter 16

WILL WAS SOUND asleep in his favorite chair on his veranda. He was not aware of the little popping noises his mouth made. They were precursors to the next phase, which would be snores. If he had learned anything in the past few years it was how to be content. Another pop escaped and Tom decided that it was enough. He crept up on his big brother, much to the delight of little Will who was watching from his crib, and stuck the end of a huge stock of wheat into Wills mouth. Unfortunately it went clear back to his cough reflex and sent Him into a coughing frenzy. By the time he got his breath the little boys were beside themselves and overcome with laughter.

"Will, why did you turn so red?" asked Tom. "I wonder why!" said Will as he grabbed his little brother and threw him over his knee. "Now see what you get." Will loved his close knit family and the beautiful valley they were so fortunate to call home. He felt fulfilled in every way. What more could he ask for? All of his dreams had come true. He had the satisfaction of watching the entire valley enterprise flourish day by day as it produced food for the needy, and work for those who would otherwise be desperate. He also watched with pride as his wife directed the education of scores of young people. This was a safe haven for not only the Indians who had fought and worked so hard to keep and develop it. It was also Will's place of refuge. There was no place on earth where he felt closer to his creator. Once again Will's thoughts drifted and he became lost in his own world. He was unaware of the young Indian brave creeping through the bushes; his face set in a mask of determination, focused only upon his unsuspecting victim.

The scuff of moccasins finally interrupted Will's reverie and he leaped out of his chair just in time to turn and catch the body hurtling towards him. There was a brief struggle, but Will quickly gained the advantage. Throwing his foe to the soft grassy ground he soon rendered him helpless. Becky and Nathan arrived just in time to save the day. "Will, you better let him up and stop tormenting him", scolded Becky. "And should I let him scalp me?" retorted Will. Terisa arrived just in time to hear Will.

"Little Hawk," she scolded "did you attack your Uncle Will again? Say good night, its time for you to come home to bed." Little Hawk was the son of Running Bird and Terisa and his name suited him perfectly. He smiled at Will and said, "I'll get you next time." Taking his mothers hand went happily home to his bed.

Nathan sat down beside Will and handed him a saddlebag. "You need to be careful son," he warned "There are still people around who would be only too glad to put a bullet in you and ride off into the sunset with this money." Will nodded at Nathan. He too knew of the dangers connected with carrying so much money. ormally they kept very little on hand but the employees of the mine were using the company more and more as a bank. They felt the big safe in the office was more secure than their homes. While they were right, it never the less put a responsibility on Will and Nathan to make sure the cash was in a safe place and that was in Yuma.

After a short conversation Will excused himself. He had a few things to do to get ready for his long ride and he wanted a good nights sleep.

He was away bright and early the next morning. It was good to get a break and be on Chalky again. He had hardly ridden him during the past several months. Will had so many memories that it was not hard to overcome the boredom of a long ride. He talked to the horse, reminding him of their adventures together; never dreaming the horse could care less. He had his own thoughts. These consisted of his favorite shade tree and the apples the little boys gave him without fail every afternoon.

Will inevitably got around to his last showdown with the Dillon's. It was relatively cut and dried. No one, including the Dillon's knew of his skill with guns and when the opportunity came Thad Dillon was not about to let it slip away.

Unfortunately Todd had not been able to break the domination of his father and found himself in a fight he wanted no part of. He determined that any shot he fired would miss, even if it cost him his life. Will had ventured into a part of Yuma he knew was not safe, but he was on a mission of mercy and the fearful but trusting eyes of the mother who had pleaded for Will's help were stronger than his sense of self preservation.

Now he must face a man who's main purpose was to end his life. The young brave he had come to rescue turned and ran leaving Will to face his enemies alone. He saw also, that those lining up to watch were sympathetic with Thad Dillon.

Wade rode away. It was a brave thing to do and when he left he didn't stop until he reached San Francisco. As a last act of defiance to his father before leaving he walked up to Will and shook his hand. He advised Will to shoot first, "and shoot to kill, because if he doesn't get you this time the next time he will shoot you in the back."

As soon as Wade was out of the line of fire Will looked at the two gunmen. "I guess if you fellows insist, we might as well get at it." With that Will drew and fired so fast that Thad and Todd were laying on the ground clutching their thighs before any one realized shots had been fired. Each of them had one bullet hole in the same spot, right through the fleshy part beside the bone. A miss in any direction could have resulted in the loss of their legs.

That was all in the past now. A part of his past that he wanted to forget. As Will rode and daydreamed, contentment was his worst enemy. He did feel a sense of uneasiness from time to time but his wishful thinking soon lulled him into complacency and his head began to gently roll forward as he dozed off.

Suddenly he was brought wide-awake by a hammer like blow in the small of the back. He hadn't heard the shot but he knew he was in trouble. He fought back the rising panic as his back and legs began to grow numb. Will spoke to Chalky who responded immediately. In an instant horse and rider were racing across the desert seeking to out-run an unseen enemy.

Thad was beside himself. Once again he had played the fool. He had shot across a deep ravine never considering the possibility that his shot wouldn't kill his man. He would just have to get across the ravine and track him down and make sure he was dead.

As for Will, he had no idea where he was or where he was heading. He realized that he was in a life and death struggle to stay on his horse. He had to put distance between himself and those who were seeking his life. He was able to sit upright long enough to use his slicker to make a cushion over his pommel. Then, with his legs nearly useless he lay forward and wrapped his arms around the horse's neck and hung on for his life.

Will woke up suddenly. Again he was forced to fight off a wave of panic that threatened to engulf him. He had to maintain his ability to think and make plans, or he would die.

He didn't know how long he had stayed on his horse, or how far they had come, or how long he had been laying on the ground. All he knew at the moment was that he was thirsty. The knowledge that he was shot came with sickening clarity as he attempted to reach the canteen attached to Chalky's saddle. With great difficulty he pulled himself up the stirrup until he reached the canteen then he eased himself back to the ground. This used up the last remaining bit of strength he had. The next thing he was aware of was the dark star filled sky above him.

Will remembered the night long ago when he lay under the same sky. That night he was filled with a sense of well being. Tonight he was bitter and lonely. He was also angry, angry with himself for being so careless and angry with God for letting this happen to him. He felt like a forgotten speck, lost and alone in the vast and hostile universe. He wanted to shout his complaint but there was no one to hear. No one cared whether he lived or died. Will was filled with fear. "Help me God," he cried out in despair.

Suddenly he saw the face of Pastor Tomkins. It was a scene from his childhood. The pastor was quoting a familiar verse from the Bible, "...I will never desert you, nor will I ever forsake you" (Hebrews 13:5 NASV). Will shut his eyes and shook his head seeking to erase the vision. "Where are you God? Where were you when I was shot?" His strength gone, he was only able to look around. He was surprised to see what looked like an adobe wall not more than eight feet from where he lay. If he could only get to it he might find shelter. If only...

The warm rays of the sun poured through the window and brought Will back to consciousness. He was surprised to find himself lying on a cot inside a stone and adobe cabin. He had spent the night in a deep-exhausted sleep, the thing he had needed the most. He also noticed that his wound had been cleaned and dressed. The feeling that someone else was there brought a cold chill. Then it dawned on Will that whoever it was must be a friend. Why patch him up then shoot him? Looking around He noticed a coffeepot on the stove. The 'fixings' lay on the table beside a couple of freshly rolled cigarettes. That and the smell of fresh tobacco told Will that his friend, whoever it was, had not gone far.

Will was frightened when Todd Dillon walked through the door. "Good morning Will." he said. Then, noticing the terror in his eyes as they searched the cabin, he continued, "I thought I would put your guns away for safe keeping."

Todd began to gently wash Will's wounds, talking to him while he worked. He didn't really talk about anything in particular. He just talked to ease the tension and help Will relax.

After feeding him Todd stopped and looked at Will. "I want you to know how sorry I am Will. I tried to stop it but I figured it out too late." Then Todd began to tremble. Hanging his head he continued, "I killed my Pa Will, I killed him." Todd broke down and sobbed. He was shedding tears of regret and remorse over his father but he was also sobbing away the years of frustration that had finally filled him up.

"I had to kill him Will, or else he would have followed you and killed you. I couldn't let him do that. You are too good of a man. I've seen God in you. It wasn't you who should die. Pa had the devil in him. He was the one who had to die." Todd poured out his heart. He accepted the guilt for his actions and talked about a longing he had felt for a long time to know the God that he saw so clearly in Will.

"I know it's too late for me but if you will only forgive me that will be enough." He finally became quiet. He looked into Will's face hoping to see forgiveness but realizing it would take all the mercy Will possessed.

"I do forgive you Todd, and it isn't too late for you with God. When Jesus hung on the cross he hung beside a thief and robber who asked Him for forgiveness. Jesus died for that robber and he died for you. Jesus paid for your sins. All you have to do is believe it and ask him to remove your guilt."

Without hesitation Todd bowed his head. "Please forgive me Jesus. I am a guilty man. I want to know you like Will does. Please make me clean."

Will was overwhelmed as he looked into the eyes of a new person. He had seen a dead man given new life. He was forced to hang his head in shame and humility. Would he be willing to suffer a gunshot wound if it meant the salvation of a soul? Jesus went to the cross without hesitation for him. Will knew he had some things to take care of with God.

Todd spent the rest of the morning making sure Will had enough supplies. He also told him about his confrontation with his father. Will knew Todd was suffering much pain, and he began to see him and Wade in a new light. The last traces of anger were swept away.

Todd intended to go and find help for Will. He thought he had a good idea where the searchers would be concentrating their efforts. Unfortunately they were not aware of the cabin since it was a hideout for outlaws. Todd was confident that Will would be safe since there were no outlaws operating in this territory at the moment.

He left in mid afternoon and Will was immediately thrown into gloom. He slept fitfully for a while then he ate the supper Todd had left him. He tried talking to God but he discovered he didn't know what to say. He decided that maybe it was God who should do the talking and he should do the listening. He felt better about that and told God that he was ready to listen. Almost instantly he was asleep. This time his sleep was invaded by a dream. In the dream a host of beings were gathered to pass judgment on the Creator of the universe. Will had been appointed judge and he was determined God would receive a fair trial. Those gathered to witness on God's behalf included Martyrs, Prophets, Patriarchs, and Apostles from every age, occupation, and nationality. Their only qualification was that they had walked with God and known Him personally during their life time.

Satan led those arrayed against God. He had gathered his forces carefully and was determined to destroy his mortal enemy. His attack was furious. "You don't keep your promises. You promised Will a bright future full of hope, and free of calamity." With a sneer and triumphant air he commanded a demon to read a statement made by God. "I know the plans that I have for you, declares the Lord, plans for welfare and not for calamity to give you a future and a hope" (Jer. 29:11).

God's answer was clear and simple, not spoken by Himself but by one of the martyrs, who had been appointed chief witness. "He never promised Will or anyone else a trouble free life". This answer was proven by Scripture. "Beloved, do not be surprised at the fiery ordeal among you, which comes for your testing, as though some strange thing were happening to you" (1 Peter 4:12). Taking the first document the demon had quoted from, the witness continued, "We must read the entire statement in question...then you will call upon me and come and pray to me, and I will listen to you. And you will seek Me and find Me, when you search for me with all your heart" (Jer. 29:12,13. NASV).

At this point the witness stood to his feet and turning to Satan asked, "Who was it that shot Will, One of God's servants or one of Satan's servants?" With his voice ringing it's authority and his eyes burning into Satan's being he continued, "It was you who tried to destroy Will, You brought calamity. It is God who provides the promise and hope through trouble and beyond to those who seek Him with all their heart."

Satan's case was shown to be weak but he plunged into his next accusation. "You left Will alone in the desert to die with no help. You broke a direct promise." Again Satan commanded one of his demons to quote, this time from the very words of Jesus. "I will not leave you comfortless: I will come to you" (John 14:18 KJV).

Once again God's witness stood to his feet, "Oh great twister of truth, you would have Will forget where his help and guidance come from. It comes by '...the Spirit of truth, whom the world cannot receive, because it does not behold Him or know Him...' Turning his gaze upon Will the witness continued, "but you know Him because He abides with you, and will be in you" (John 14:17 NASV). Looking deep into Will's soul the witness said, "He is always with you. You know that"

The witness turned from Will and looked directly at Satan with an authority that could only come from the very Throne of God. "I have one more short statement to read, made from the cross by the one you were seeking to destroy and who has promised to be with those who will trust Him. These words seal your fate." He held a scroll bearing the inscription 'Words that cannot be denied,' and from it read, "It is finished!" Then, with eyes that seemed to sear the very soul of Satan, he shouted, "Your doom has been sealed!"

This was too much for Satan and he fled the courtroom amid the cheers and hallelujahs of the throng of witnesses and onlookers. Will woke with a start. The sun was just coming up. He felt more rested, and strangely, more at peace. As he lay staring out the door the dream came back to him little by little. Each lesson and truth, he tucked in his heart. He still had questions though and felt he deserved some reasons. All his life Will had lived by a code of fairness. Now he couldn't see any fairness to what was happening to him. How could he square it with his beliefs? How could he give up his beliefs?

About noon he heard horses. Still unable to use his legs he positioned himself on the cot so that he could use his guns, then he waited to see who would come through the door. Once again Will came to the end of his strength. Sweat started to trickle down his neck as he fought the weakness and fatigue overtaking him. His gun began to grow heavy and difficult to hold steady. The cabin door began to dance and shimmer, and then it began to recede as if entering a tunnel. He must stay awake. He mustn't allow the darkness to close in on him. His body began to quake and he fought the fear seeking to overtake him as he felt the control of his arms and hands slipping away. The last thing that went through his head as he slipped into oblivion was that he was at the mercy of those coming through the door.

Chapter 17

ECKY FROZE AT the sight before her. Will lay unconscious, his skin the color of death. She could only stare as Dr. Cully frantically searched for signs of life. After a moment he turned to Becky, his eyes full of gratitude. "He has a good even pulse. I think he has a chance." Becky collapsed on the floor and wept.

They had been searching for him for two days, along with several others who had formed small search parties. When they met Todd Dillon he told them where to find Will and expressed concern for him. It was a concern he had not had the heart to share with Will. He had seen that kind of wound before and he had never seen one turn out well for the victim. He also told them a horrible tale. He was surprised when his father ambushed Will and decided he was not going to allow him to track him down and finish the job. When he tried to block his way they fought it out in the desert until Todd was forced to kill his father or be killed. Todd was full of remorse and begged for a chance to help.

Terisa got busy lighting a signal fire and the Doctor began working on Will, cleaning and examining the wound. It was an ugly red with inflammation and his body was hot with fever. He couldn't understand why there was so little damage from the gunshot itself.

The bullet was still in his back and a gun of that caliber should have ripped right through him rather than lodge itself as it did. He finally understood when Terisa called his attention to Chalky's saddle. The bullet had hit the back of the seat then ricocheted and struck Will's back. The saddle had absorbed its power.

The doctor insisted that they wait at least one day before trying to move Will. He needed to gain some strength and he was also dehydrated. Will slept most of the day. Every time he opened his eyes he looked into those of Becky who never left his side. He would smile and drift off to sleep again, thanking his Maker for such a faithful wife.

The next morning they bundled Will into a wagon that had been brought to transport him. Blankets and pillows were piled on a bed of straw to soften his ride. The ground was rough and the constant jostling caused considerable pain so they were forced to stop often to give Will relief. The hours passed and the day wore on. Finally the Doctor announced they must stop and rest for the night.

After darkness had overtaken them Will and Becky lay side by side looking up at the stars. Will talked to Becky about the night so long ago, with Nathan, out in the desert looking at these same stars. Things had changed so much. Then, his world was filled with so much promise. Now it was full of doubt and uncertainty.

Becky gently scolded him. "What was his promise based upon back then? The stars and moon are still here, and the one who put them in their place is still here. As far as I know, He hasn't cancelled His love or any of His promises. And He hasn't forgotten who Will Carter is either."

Will considered Becky's words as she drifted off to sleep. Her question burned into his soul. "What was your promise based upon?" Will began to realize that he must base all hope and every promise upon something which is permanent in itself.

He had lots of time to reflect on how circumstances change, and how you can't depend on them. Friends sometimes let you down. He spoke to himself about Becky. "I can always count on her." But he realized that even though she was true and faithful she was as vulnerable as he was.

Will had always seen the heavens as a symbol of God's greatness. Becky had said, "The stars and moon are still here." It dawned on him that they were nothing more than matter, put in place for a purpose, and devoid of life of their own. That left only one person, the Creator. It came, at first quietly then with a rush of emotion, the realization that he had been trusting in the gifts of God for his security rather than the giver of these gifts. If one failed he could always switch. Something or someone had always been there for him. And all the time he thought he was trusting God.

Will fell into a peaceful sleep. Almost immediately he began to dream. He dreamt he was walking toward a hill with three strange looking trees on it. The peace he had felt began to diminish as he neared the hill and saw that the trees were really crosses. His blood began to chill as he realized one of the persons on the cross, looked like him. He unconsciously began to slow his steps, then he saw the face of Jesus and the words "I have been crucified with Christ," (Gal. 2:20) written on a board and tacked to the cross.

It was as though Jesus was inviting him to join in His suffering. Will suddenly found himself on the cross. As he looked into the eyes of Jesus he saw something he had never seen before. Rather than mercy and pity, and forgiveness, he saw a look of respect like someone would feel toward a comrade or a valued friend.

For the first time in his life Will realized how important suffering was. It dawned on him that everything accomplished that was worthwhile involved suffering. At that point Jesus drew his attention to a column of men and women marching toward the cross. At the head of the column marched a young boy wearing a martyr's crown and carrying a sign which read "**Those of whom the world was not worthy**"

Jesus looked at them with obvious love and said, "These are the greatest of all My kingdom. I have no better friends than these." There followed a long line of ordinary men and women who obviously had suffered greatly, giving their very lives. The question was clear to Will. Are you willing to suffer to accomplish the will of the Creator when you may not even know what that will is?

Will looked into the eyes of Jesus but he had to look away. He wanted to say yes but his soul was filled with questions and they began to spill out. "Why are you still on the cross Jesus?" "How can evil be destroyed by a foe who yields to pain and defeat?" "What will my unnecessary suffering accomplish?"

The questions came one after another until Will finally noticed that he was no longer on the cross. With each question he found himself father away from Jesus and the Heroes. Finally in desperation he shouted, "I need to know why!" The face of Jesus turned to a mask of grief and Will was filled with panic as the scene receded and faded from his view.

He woke to find himself soaking wet. The peace he had experienced before going to sleep was gone and he was now filled with emotions he could not control or eliminate. For the first time in his life he felt himself separated from God. Part of him knew it was his fault and part of him blamed God. In his innermost being he knew he was beginning a battle that would set the course for the remainder of his life.

His eyes fell on the woman next to him. He was filled with love for her yet he knew she was not capable of meeting his deepest needs, nor could he hers. Will Carter fell asleep realizing he had no choice but to come to terms with his Maker. The question was How?

Chapter 18

WILL WAS GLAD to be home, though he churned with inner turmoil and was beset by issues only he could deal with. They were too painful and personal to share with anyone else. He had no desire to discuss them with the valley Pastor or even with Pastor Tomkins. Dr. Cully seemed to understand better than the others and he chose to keep quiet. He did, however take the time to help Will identify the areas of battle.

As he finished changing Will's dressings he began to talk to him. "Will, I want you to listen to what I have to say. You are of no help to yourself or your wife until you deal with a few issues. First of all we have to get your wound healed. That will be relatively simple. Time will take care of that, and time will also tell us how much damage has been done. You have another wound that will kill you if you don't get it healed, the wound in your soul."

Will knew what his friend was talking about. He felt betrayed by God and he had lost his sense of direction. His future, which had always been so promising, was now bleak. He was haunted by the dreams he had experienced while out in the desert waiting for help, quite aware of their implications. Part of him was settled and ready to get on with life. Another part of him was governed by fear for the future and inability to trust his Creator. The two sides of him prepared to fight it out.

To most people Will seemed at peace. They didn't realize he was dealing with mental as well as physical pain. The hardest thing to contend with was the knowledge he was a cripple, and would probably remain so. The bullet was lodged against his spinal cord and any movement caused pain. The best he could hope for was that medicine would advance to the point that the bullet could be removed. That would require new techniques and knowledge, and Will knew medical science moved slowly.

There was much for Will to get used to. Instead of going to work every morning his days were dedicated to regaining his strength and restoring his general health. Becky left her job and devoted herself to caring for him. For his part he was determined to do as much for himself as possible. He was also determined to broaden his horizons and stretch himself to the limit of his physical capabilities.

Will was young and strong and his efforts paid off. His arms, and upper body strengthened so that he gained greater agility and mobility. Becky was always there to encourage him. She was especially proud the night he surprised everyone by walking unaided onto the veranda with his crutches. It was painful and slow but Will brimmed with hope.

There was another factor that fired Will's determination and added hope to his life. That was his son Little Will. He was only a year old at the time of the shooting incident but even at such a young age he was capable of receiving and giving much love. Will had been so excited on the day of his birth. It always brought a smile when he thought back. Becky woke him up early, before daylight. Will had determined before hand that he would not become incoherent like Nathan had at his sons birth.

Unfortunately He experienced a condition The Dr. called 'sympathy pains'. While determined to be supportive and helpful he became, as his wife put it, "a pain in the neck."

Becky later described the birthing process. First there was the pains. Will's corresponded perfectly with hers, pain for pain; breath for breath Then came the sweating and the bearing down. Will did display one thing missing in Becky's experience, pure horror. By the time the baby was coming Will was reduced to sitting on a chair outside Becky's room with his face in his hands. The cry of his newborn son brought a flood of joy and love. Looking into the perfect little face Will said to himself, "What a God I worship. Surly the God who is able to make such a beautiful child will continue to bless him all of his days."

Later as Will looked back upon this incident, it became a great source of encouragement that drew him back to his earlier faith.

He was soon working part time at the mine and the highlight of each day was the ride he took with Becky to survey the valley in their little buckboard. Running Bird had fit it with especially soft springs so that instead of injuring Wills back it actually worked to message and strengthen it.

One day as Will watched his son play on the veranda he heard two horses approach. A few minutes later Running Bird appeared. "Will, there are a couple of fellows who would like to talk to you if you will allow them to". Will was a little puzzled because people didn't usually ask permission to talk to him. "Sure, who are they?" he asked. "Todd and Wade" replied Running Bird.

Will gave an involuntary start as the memories flooded in on him. He was a little hesitant to let them see him in the condition he was in. Sensing his struggle, Running Bird explained that they had gone to Sheriff Moore and confessed their crimes and were determined to make restitution where at all possible. Their trial was coming up soon and they wanted to see him in case they were sent to prison.

Tension filled the air as the two men approached Will. Todd was speechless with remorse and Wade was nearly overcome by the sight of his life long adversary in this condition. After an agonizing minute in which no one spoke, Will thrust out his hand and they both eagerly stepped forward and shook hands with him. The first thing Will did was to thank Todd for saving his life The floodgates were then opened and both men allowed the words to flow seeking forgiveness and attempting to somehow show Will how sorry they were.

Wade confessed that each time they fought, he respected Will more, until the respect displaced the hate. Now he just desired to be a friend but he knew that was not possible. Will looked at them both with a stern look that didn't quite match the sudden twinkle in his eyes. "Well boys, I think I would rather have you as friends than enemies. It would make life a lot simpler."

Later, after they were gone Will knew that a great burden had been removed. He no longer had to contend with the emotions that constantly tried to divert him. The temptation to hate them and seek revenge, and the smoldering instinct to constantly look over his shoulder were all removed by the simple act of reconciliation and forgiveness. One more obstacle to rebuilding his life was removed.

Will knew he had more lessons to learn and much understanding to gain in many areas and issues that he had never dreamed of before being shot. He was a good learner and knew enough to take things one at a time. Becky and Will's friends watched as he returned more and more to the man he used to be. Things were going so well that no one was prepared for what was to come.

One evening Will felt unusually tired so he went to bed early. By midnight he was soaked in perspiration and delirious. Dr. Cully was awakened by the panic stricken voice of Becky. "Will's dying", she sobbed. Dr. Cully was frightened. Becky never panicked. He wasted no time getting to Will.

The news was not good. The thing he had feared the most had come to pass. Will had a bad infection that threatened to take his life. Even if he could pull him through it was doubtful that he would ever walk again, even with crutches.

Will fought gallantly as those closest to him stood by, able only to pray. After several weeks he began to heal, but all he had won before was lost. This time he had new enemies, discouragement and bitterness. He felt like a prisoner helpless and alone with no good reason to go on. The one person Will felt free to share his innermost feelings with was Running Bird. Now he began to pour them out with no mercy. Running Bird tried to understand and be patient but he finally could stand no more.

"I never thought I would see the day that you gave in to self pity" he growled. "What are you talking about?" asked Will his face turning

bright red.

"Why don't you just stand up and face things like a man?" "Well friend it just so happens I can't stand up!"

"You know what I mean!" retorted Running Bird. "And don't forget the people whose happiness depends on how you handle this little setback."

"A fine friend you are" retorted Will. "You're a regular Jobs comforter." Running Bird quietly said, "Why don't you read about Job? Maybe you will learn something." Will took the challenge. It didn't go well at first. His anger only grew as he read about the conversations between God and Satan. He felt it was entirely unfair, that they were using him as bargaining a chip. It wasn't long before he began to see himself as another Job sitting at the garbage heap scratching himself and demanding answers. He protested his innocence of any great sin and felt he was the victim of indifference.

Will knew deep within himself that he was wrong but he couldn't seem to rid himself of his anger. After all God had abandoned Job, the most faithful of men for no good reason. Then he left him, to suffer all alone, never once answering the man's cries.

There came a day when Will knew it was time to finally settle things once and for all. When bedtime came he refused to go to bed. Becky was mildly shocked. "Where are you going to stay?"

"Right here on the veranda." Becky knew there was no use arguing with him so she made sure he had everything he would need within reach and went off to bed.

It wasn't long before Will felt the loneliness. Darkness closed around him but he set his jaw in stubborn defiance. He heard the rustle of a busy family of mice. He didn't mind them. It was the bats that swooped down ever closer to his head that sent shivers down his back. Later he was even visited by a curious doe but he heard nothing from God. Will stubbornly refused to utter a word. All night he sat soundlessly waiting for God to explain Himself. Not a word was heard from God but Will couldn't rid his mind of the image of the beautiful sunset he witnessed the night before. It was as if God was speaking to him but he stubbornly held out, refusing to listen or respond to the master designer.

Just as the sky began a subtle change Will's eyelids became just too heavy and he began to slide into sleep. He sensed more than saw a sudden green glow the shape of a sun peeking over the horizon at him, then came a deep crimson that began to splash itself over the eastern sky. Will witnessed the most beautiful sunrise he had ever seen.

This was just too much. God was not playing fair. Livid with anger Will could finally contain himself no longer. "How can a God who can create such beauty, and who holds the universe together without effort allow good people to suffer?"

Almost as an afterthought, as the world around him came to life, he took his Bible and began reading the account of Job's meeting with God. He was overwhelmed as he saw the greatness of creation and he shuddered with Job as he saw God in His majesty. His heart almost exploded as it dawned on him that not one of Job's questions were answered.

He gasped for breath as the truth rolled over him like a crashing sea wave that left him awash and at the mercy of it's controlling power; What right did he have to demand answers? As he saw the God of the universe, whose ways were so far above and beyond his own, he knew he had only one option and only one plea. He hoped he had not presumed too long on the mercy of God.

Bowing his head he joined with Job. "I have heard of thee by the hearing of the ear; But now my eye sees thee. Therefore I retract, and I repent in dust and ashes." Job 42:5,6 NASV. There were two other sets of eyes that had not closed all night. One set blinked in satisfaction and retired into the stronghold of eternity. The other set closed, awash in the tears of gratitude, and enjoyed the sleep of a wife who's faith was rewarded.

❧ ❦

A beautiful afternoon found Will at his favorite pastime, sitting on the veranda with Becky, enjoying the beautiful view of the valley and watching his son Little Will play. During these times he and Becky felt a special bond that enabled them to share their deepest cares and feelings. On this particular occasion Terisa and Running Bird, as well as Helen and Nathan were there also. They were engaged in small talk and enjoying Nathan's humor, mostly at the expense of Will. It was one of those evenings when the warm breezes wafting off of the valley floor carried the sweet aroma of ripening citrus. An occasional shooting star punctuated the peace and made everything right.

Suddenly during a lull in the banter, Running Bird said "There was a time not long ago that I thought I would never see you like this again, enjoying the company of your family and friends. Tell us your secret Will." Will thought a moment and said, "I have learned so much. Probably the most important thing I've discovered is that everything God allows in my life is tempered by His love. So I can face anything if I do it one day at a time trusting in God's integrity. This enables me to keep from being overwhelmed and allows me to develop a strategy for living. It has also freed me to understand other secrets of living with pain and disappointment."

Terisa reached over and touched his hand. Please tell us

About them will. For the next hour Will shared the secrets with those who loved him most. He told how he had learned to reject guilt for not being able to do the things he once could do. It was such a relief when he understood that new circumstances brought new responsibilities. God had new expectations that were within Will's capabilities. From that discovery came the ability to focus on the right things and the right person.

There were too many things seeking to divert his attention, inviting comparisons that were unnecessary, and only brought disappointment and confusion.

Will went on, telling how he had thought back to the day he rescued Terisa. His perspective from the high vantage point, while giving the necessary information to carry out his plan, was still very limited compared to God's perspective, which is totally unlimited. As a result he didn't need to understand every thing. He learned to take comfort in the answers he did have while trusting in the faithfulness of his creator for the questions he could find no answers for.

"Terisa referred to me as a friend of God. This made me ashamed of myself because I was at best a terrible friend. Friendship is a two-way road. Jesus died for His friends while they denied him and deserted Him. That didn't keep Him from dying for them. He didn't do it because they deserved it. And it wasn't because they were such good friends because they weren't. He did it because he loved them. He said I could be His friend.

Honesty and trust characterize a good friendship. I need to learn how to trust Him. He's always honest with me." "Isaiah 55:8,9 tells me that His ways and His thoughts are so much higher than mine that I can't expect to understand everything. Some day I will know when the time is right."

Reaching over and taking Becky's hand he continued, "until then we will continue enjoying the good things we have been blessed with right now." After Will finished there was a long silence as his friends thought about what he had said.

The reverie came to an abrupt end by the somewhat noisy approach of Dr. Cully. His face was stern and business like. "I'm glad I found you all together because I am about to make my last medical diagnosis, then I am retiring for good. This is getting to be too much for me." Looking gravely at Will the Doctor continued, "Will you may as well get used to this now, your going to be a father again." With that the old gentleman turned and walked into the evening. As he walked he began to laugh, first softly then with more and more enthusiasm, until his laughter resounded through out the valley of refuge.

THE END